LIVE
THROUGH
THIS

Also by Mindi Scott

Freefall

LIVE THROUGH THIS

MINDI SCOTT

SIMON PULSE

NEW YORK LONDON TORONTO SYDNEY NEW DELHI

SIMON PULSE

An imprint of Simon & Schuster Children's Publishing Division

1230 Avenue of the Americas, New York, NY 10020

First Simon Pulse edition October 2012

Copyright © 2012 by Mindi Scott

All rights reserved, including the right of reproduction in whole or in part in any form.

SIMON PULSE and colophon are registered trademarks of Simon & Schuster, Inc.

For information about special discounts for bulk purchases,

please contact Simon & Schuster Special Sales at 1-866-506-1949

or business@simonandschuster.com.

The Simon & Schuster Speakers Bureau can bring authors to your live event.

For more information or to book an event contact

the Simon & Schuster Speakers Bureau at 1-866-248-3049

or visit our website at www.simonspeakers.com.

Designed by Hilary Zarycky

The text of this book was set in Fairfield.

Manufactured in the United States of America

2 4 6 8 10 9 7 5 3 1

Library of Congress Cataloging-in-Publication Data

Scott, Mindi.

Live through this / Mindi Scott.

p. cm.

Summary: From the outside, fifteen-year-old Coley Sterling's life seems imperfect but normal, but for years she has buried her shame and guilt over a relationship that crossed the line, and now that she has a chance at having a real boyfriend, Reece, the lies begin to unravel.

[1. Dating (Social customs)—Fiction. 2. Secrets—Fiction. 3. Sexual abuse—Fiction.

4. Incest—Fiction. 5. Stepfamilies—Fiction.

6. Family life—Washington (State)—Fiction.] I. Title.

PZ7.S42738Liv 2012 [Fic]—dc23 2012006006

ISBN 978-1-4424-4059-3 (hc)

ISBN 978-1-4424-4060-9 (pbk)

ISBN 978-1-4424-4061-6 (eBook)

For Ella, Cadence, and Brody

ACKNOWLEDGMENTS

My husband, Dwayne Scott, gets top billing here for always answering "yes" to the question "Can you take another look at this scene for me?" I am thankful for your skills at alternating between being my devoted teammate, stern coach, and diehard fan, depending upon what I need on any given writing day. Olive you, every second. Also? Clear eyes, full hearts, can't lose!

Thank you to my editor, Liesa Abrams, and my agent, Jim McCarthy, for completely believing in this book and for sending me e-mails that made me cry in a good way. Working with you both is an honor and a pleasure, and I feel lucky *every single day* that you're on my side.

I also very much appreciate those who work behind the scenes at Simon & Schuster, as well as everyone who assisted me with research, brainstorming, critiques, and/or sanity preservation: Adrienne Fox, Andrea Perrin (still Seth's #1 fan!),

Angela Johnson, Brandy Colbert, Brandy Stockwell, Bryan Larson, Diana Jeong, Donna Ballman, Jamie Cross, Joyce Huttula, Justin Ordonez, Kari Olson, Laura Capinha, Leeann Ward, Dr. Linda Young, Lindsey Schoenberger, Marcia Kelly-Gerritz, Marie Gahler, Melanie Turner, Michelle Andreani, Nikki Thompson, Ruth Gallogly, and the Tenners.

And finally, a million, billion thank-yous to my family, friends, and all of the other wonderful people out there who read *Freefall* and helped to spread the word. I am so grateful for your love and support. xoxo

LIVE THROUGH THIS

CHAPTER 1

I'm on my bed, under the covers, and my boyfriend is kissing my neck. He lifts my shirt, lowers his face. My heart is beating, beating, beating. I want him to do more, go further. I don't tell him—I don't say anything at all—but he figures it out and slides his hand way down. My whole body is on fire in the best possible way. Especially there. Right *there*. I tug on his boxers and he sighs.

I start awake.

A hint of cologne. Soft breathing. Darkness. It's real. This is all happening. But not with the imaginary boyfriend from my dream.

My hands, my arms, my frame go limp. His fingers keep doing what they're doing. Soon this will be over. I keep my eyes shut and hold my breath while the wave builds and builds and builds and builds and *then*—the wonderful, terrible crash.

It doesn't matter that I tried not to tense up; he knows.

Somehow, he's always been able to tell. Gently, he kisses my cheek. Then he stands, straightens my blankets, and closes the door behind him.

I press my pillow onto my face and wish that it were possible to suffocate myself.

CHAPTER 2

In the morning, my shower is extra-long. It's an ongoing joke in my family that I take forever and ever to get ready, but today is truly epic. Just looking at myself in the mirror requires extreme effort.

As I'm finishing blow-drying, I notice a red splotch on my neck: a real-life, actual hickey. Holding back tears, I separate my blond hair into sections and use my huge curling iron to get it all sleek. With shaking hands, I touch the scalding metal barrel to my skin for a fraction of a second—just enough time to cover the mark with an inch-long burn.

I make my way upstairs. As usual, the triplets—my nine-year-old half brothers and half sister—are up before they need to be, watching cartoons in their pajamas, and arguing.

Jacob: ". . . That's because Leonardo is the best Ninja Turtle and you *know* it!"

Emma: "No, he isn't."

Zach: "Jacob, you're stupid."

Jacob: "Shut up. *You're* stupid."

Down the hall, my mom and stepdad's conversation is equally ordinary.

Tony: ". . . No late appointments today, so I'll be home right after I'm done with my three o'clock."

Mom: "Dinner at six, then? Or six thirty?"

Tony: "Six should work."

Mom: "Good. It's hard to make the kids wait after karate."

All these normal conversations in my normal house with my not-as-normal-as-everyone-thinks family are making me dizzy.

Usually, I eat breakfast at the table, but Reece will be here very soon, so I grab an apple and a cheese stick from the fridge, as well as a water bottle and a granola bar to put in my dance cooler. Without a word to anyone, I rush outside, down the steps, across the street.

It's raining. I set my gym bag at my feet. I eat my cheese and wait.

Everything's gray this winter morning: my jacket, our house, the sky, the street. Even the things that usually have color—grass, evergreens, other houses, my shoes—are under a haze somehow.

Our garage door opens and Tony backs the Lexus out of

the driveway. He pulls up next to me and lowers the passenger-side window. "Do you need me to drive you to school, Coley?" he asks, leaning across the seat and smiling at me in his caffeinated, morning-person way.

"No. My ride's going to be here in a minute."

"Who? That Reece kid?"

I don't answer; I'm not getting into this with him.

Shaking his gray and silver head, Tony opens the glove box. He grabs his mini-umbrella and holds it out the window toward me. "Here you go. I know how you feel about your hair."

I want to refuse the stupid thing, but that isn't going to make him leave, so I just take it.

He smiles again, not quite as brightly as before. "See you at dinner. It's taco night and your mom's going to see if she can get Bryan to make his world-famous salsa. Woo hoo!"

I busy myself with opening the umbrella so I don't have to acknowledge Tony and his corniness as he drives away.

After about two minutes, Reece shows up in his little blue Toyota truck. He parks in front of me on the side of the road. The wipers scrape across the windshield, over his face. Back and forth, back and forth, back and forth. He's looking at me the way he does every morning: like he's glad I exist, like he feels lucky to hang out with a girl like me.

My stomach twists. He has *no* idea.

Leaving the engine running, he jumps out and jogs around the truck. "Am I late or something?"

I have the strangest urge to throw myself at him, to put my face against his chest and tell him everything. I can't do that, though. Not ever.

"You're right on time. I just wanted to *not* keep you waiting for once," I say, focusing on closing Tony's umbrella in order to avoid Reece's gaze.

He opens my door, flips the seat forward, and pushes my stuff in next to his under the jump seats. "Hey, Coley. Have I ever told you you're my hero and everything I would like to be?"

On any other day, I might have found it funny. For the past few weeks, we've been playing this game where one of us gives an over-the-top compliment by quoting lyrics, and then the other guesses who performed the song. For once, I'm not tempted to crack a smile or play along. I just get into the truck.

Reece walks back around to the driver's side and sits beside me. "Bette Midler. I don't know why, but I thought for sure you'd get that." He steers us out of the neighborhood and onto the main street, and then clears his throat. "So I have something *awesome* to tell you. My grandparents decided to stay with us only through Christmas. The day after, they're heading to Portland to see my aunt and uncle. We'll go down there for New Year's a few days later."

I can't guess why this is so exciting to him, but I can tell from his voice that I'm supposed to feel the same way. "Oh?"

"Yeah! We found out last night, and my parents finally caved and said that I can meet up with you guys."

I glance over at him. "Meet up with who?"

"Um. Your family. At Whistler? You did invite me on your snowboarding trip, right? Or . . . not?"

"*Oh!* Yes. I did."

But really, I didn't. What I'd said is it would be fun if we went snowboarding together. And by that, I'd meant that we should go for a day at, like, Crystal or Snoqualmie Pass, not that he should come on vacation in Canada with my entire household.

"Okay," he says. "So I can get up there the day before you come home. And my mom is going to call your mom. Probably today or tomorrow or something. Just to make sure it's all on the up and up. Because she's like that."

My mom's the same way, and my accidental invitation isn't going to go over well. Mom and Tony are going to say no and then I'll have to tell Reece and then he'll think that they don't like him. And he'll be right. Not because there's anything *not* to like about him, but because he's a boy and they happen to be strict about boys.

I slump in my seat.

Reece goes on. "I'll probably just drive up to BC really early that morning. How long's the drive? Five hours?"

"I think so."

"Cool. But you're not going to take me on hard trails first thing, right? I read that the double black diamonds at Whistler and Blackcomb are the real deal. In other words, suicide."

"I don't go on double diamonds."

He motions as if to wipe his forehead. "Phew."

I turn away and stare at the never-ending grayness outside my raindrop-covered window. My eyes threaten to get teary, but I won't let it happen.

No.

No.

The truck coasts to the bottom of the hill that separates our town into two sections, through the intersection that leads to school, and finally, into Reece's assigned spot in the Kenburn High parking lot. He turns off the engine, but neither of us makes a move to get out.

"Is something wrong?" he asks. "You don't seem like yourself this morning."

I stare at my hands on my lap, at his hands still on the steering wheel. I breathe in. Out. "I didn't get a lot of sleep last night."

"Are you sure that's what it is? Because, I mean, you're allowed to change your mind about the trip, you know."

"No, I want you to come with us." It physically hurts, deep inside my chest, but I look into his eyes anyway. "I mean it."

And I do. I really, really do. Somehow, someway, I'll make it happen.

We walk toward the school, umbrella-less. Me, holding my gym bag stuffed with clothes and books. Him, lugging his saxophone case and slouching under the too-loose straps of his backpack.

Over the gray, under the gray, through the gray.

Snap out of it, Coley.

Deep breath.

Last night wasn't real. It didn't happen.

Deep breath.

It was a nightmare. Just another screwed-up dream.

Deep breath.

None of it has ever happened. This. Right now. This is what's real.

Deep breath.

This is my life.

Slooooow exhale.

I lift my chin and put my shoulders back.

Just like always, Reece holds the door for me and we make

our way inside where lockers are slamming and dozens of conversations are in progress. Just like always, I wave and say "hi" as I pass friends. At the second corridor, we pause and Reece looks down at me.

"See you at lunch?" I ask, flashing a dance-competition-worthy smile.

He smiles back—relieved, I think. "Yes, you will."

This is what I do; it's what I'm good at. I was voted "Freshman Girl—Best Smile" last year for legitimate reasons.

I go my way and he goes his. But after about ten feet, I remember something important. "Hey, Reece?"

"Yeah?" he asks, turning.

"Have I ever told you that you're just like an angel and your skin makes me cry?"

He laughs. "That's by . . . Radiohead?"

I nod and dance away.

This is my life.

CHAPTER 3

At the end of the day, I rush to Gym B and drop my bag and poms by the wall. I'm always the first to arrive for dance practice now that I change in the bathroom between fifth and sixth period. My avoiding-the-locker-room situation isn't ideal, but it's necessary to keep peace on the team.

"All by yourself again, Sterling?" Josh calls out as he and three other guys from the wrestling team head toward their mats. "Where are all the other hot cheerleaders?"

Boys who call me by my last name are almost as annoying as the ones who can't tell the difference between dancers and cheerleaders, but I know that this one is teasing me.

"Cheerleaders in *here*?" I say, looking around. "I've never seen such a thing. But maybe you can tell me where the rest of your fellow gymnasts are?"

He shakes his head and we both laugh.

The partition between Gym A and Gym B is still open, and

I spot Noah over on his side with a few of the other basketball players, warming up. It's loud already with balls bouncing and rubber soles screeching over the floor. I have a couple of minutes before my practice officially begins, so I jog over to him.

Noah's red-brown hair is flattened onto his forehead from wearing a hat all day. He shoots from the free-throw line and makes it. "Oh, there you are," he says. "I was just thinking how very sad it is that I haven't seen you since fifth period."

I make a run for his ball. "Yes, it feels like an eternity for me, too."

We've never planned it, but Noah and I end up in almost all of the same classes every year. It's been this way since kindergarten. This semester, we're together for everything except math sixth period—and that's just because he's so much better with numbers than most sophomores.

I try to take a shot from outside, but Noah blocks it easily and stands dribbling beside me. "I was delivered tragic news that my sister's having one of her girly parties tonight," he says. "You're coming this time, right?"

"Unless my mom pulls an unexpected 'family night' demand. And she might since Bryan's home from college and everything."

"No family night allowed," he says, shaking his head. "You need to be at my house so that no crazy shit goes down."

I tilt my head like I'm confused, but I know way more about what happened two weeks ago with Noah and Kimber than I'll ever let on to him. "What do you mean? Give me an example of something crazy that would happen in my absence."

"Just be there, Coley. You know you want to."

I smile. "I'll see what I can do."

He shoots and *swish*! "Piper must not know that Bryan's home because the angsting hasn't started yet."

I gaze toward Gym B where Piper—Noah's older sister, who also happens to be my squad captain—is doing splits. "Maybe she's finally over him?"

"Doubtful," he says.

"Hey, Crowne!" the head basketball coach calls out. "Your girlfriend's joining us?"

Noah yells back, "No way, Coach! She likes being on a *winning* team."

Coach Hutchinson points to the ground in front of him. "Get over here. *Now*. And your smart mouth just earned you an extra thirty laps after practice."

"Uh, gotta go," Noah says, giving me a quick wink before he runs off.

If Coach Laine ever became as mad at me as Noah's coach gets at him, I'd be a wreck. Of course, I would never give her a reason to.

I rush to my own side of the gym and slip through right before a few players pull the partition shut. Most of my teammates have set their things down near mine to get warmed up. Ming and Dia are running laps, so I hurry over to them. Dia's curly, dark hair is pulled into a French braid, but Ming's shiny black ponytail swings wildly left to right with every move she makes.

"Wow, that's some distracting hair," I say in a stern voice like Coach Laine's. "Points off for you, chickadee."

Dia scoots over so that I can jog between them. Ming flicks at my tight hair bun.

"Coley, we were just dissecting you," Dia says.

"That sounds gross. I'm glad I missed it."

Ming nudges my arm. "Don't look now. Alejandra's totally giving us the evil eye."

I don't look. I never look Alejandra's way if I can help it.

"Hey, wait a sec," Ming says. "What's that on your neck?"

My back stiffens, but I force a laugh. "Oh, this? Just a hickey."

"*What?*" Dia and Ming shriek at the same time.

I laugh again—for real this time. "I'm totally kidding. It's from my curling iron. Slippery thing."

"Listen up, girls!" Coach Laine calls out from behind us. "Yes, this is the last school day of the year, but we've got a tough workout today. So don't be acting like you're already on winter break!"

We pick up the pace.

"Just two more hours," Dia says.

"And then two glorious weeks of freedom," Ming says.

"I can't *wait*," I say.

Our twenty-member dance team is pretty much run like boot camp and we work harder than most sports teams at school. There are plenty of times when we complain about how tough it is having two-hour weekday and four-hour Saturday practices all school year. But the truth is, whenever we rock a performance or win a competition, we know without a doubt that it's all worth it. Still, I've been counting down the days until this vacation, and I'm relieved that it's finally almost here.

We finish a few more laps, and then Ming, Dia, and I sit on the floor for stretches.

Dia and I both turn at the waist and look over our shoulders, facing each other. "Don't you want to hear what Ming and I were saying about you?" she asks.

I'm not sure I do, but I twist the other way toward Ming and say, "You know it."

"Well," Dia says. "We were talking about you and Noah, of course—"

"There is no me and Noah," I say, for probably the three billionth time since seventh grade.

"And that's good," Ming says, "because you and Noah hooking up would be practically incestuous."

"Eww," Dia and I say together.

Ming goes on. "I'm trying to figure out what exactly is going on with you and that certain someone you've been eating lunch with in the band room."

My heart jumps, but I try not to let on. "I don't know what you're talking about."

"No?" Ming smiles slyly. "True or false? A tall, super-skinny tenor-sax player is going on vacation with you and your family."

I can't even try to deny it; Ming's boyfriend, Xander, happens to be friends with Reece, and is the likeliest source of her information.

Keeping my legs straight in front of me on the floor, I lean over my knees and reach to hold on to my feet. "You know, I could probably answer your question better if I had any idea what a tenor sax even is."

Dia snort-laughs. "It's the instrument that Reece Kinsey plays. But something tells me you already knew that."

"Oh, right. The answer is 'maybe true.' But jeez—he isn't *that* skinny." I lift my head in time to see Ming and Dia exchange grins. If my arms were long enough, I'd give them each a push. "He might meet us up there for the last couple of days," I say. "It isn't a big deal."

"Maybe not to *you*," Ming says.

I want to ask her what she means—she thinks it's a big deal, or Reece does?—but Coach Laine chooses that moment to get things started. "On your feet, everyone."

We split into our squads. Like always, Alejandra frowns when Ming, Dia, and I come over to her and Hannah, but it isn't like we have any more choice in this than she has.

Piper stands in front of us with her hands clasped behind her back. In her squad-captain voice, she says, "I think I have fixes for the kinks in our new routine. Let's try it out today, okay?"

So we do. We spend two hours synchronizing arms, legs, bodies, heads, hands, feet, props. Two hours mixing in the right kicks, high kicks, leg lifts, splits, jump splits. Two hours stopping and starting, stopping and starting, trying this and trying that. We work it, and we work it, and we work it some more.

Five. Six. Seven. Eight. One. Two. Three. Four.

Clap, clap, clap, clap. Clap, clap, clap, clap.

Just when I've had too much, when I'm sure that my legs will give way if I have to do *one more* high kick, Piper tells us to "*Keep going!*"

Don't stop. Let's go, let's go. Get it right, get it right, get it right. Higher, higher, higher, higher. Kick, kick, kick, kick, kick.

I do everything she says, when she says it, how she says it. She knows what we're capable of better than we do. She knows how to make us push through and never stop until long after every wrestler has cleared out, until we've given everything we can, until the end of practice finally comes.

"All right, chickadees," Coach Laine yells. "That's that. Now grab your water and let's have a seat."

"Time for another inspirational circle time," Ming says, panting a little.

Everyone on the team drags themselves to the center of the gym and plops down—red-faced and sweaty—in a half circle around Coach Laine. I hold my metal bottle against my cheek to cool down. Next to me, Piper smooths back a few of her auburn strands, which came loose during our workout.

Coach gets right to it. "This winter break is going to be a vacation in the sense that no practices are scheduled. But it is absolutely not an excuse to take a vacation from taking care of yourselves. Competition season is on the way, and starting in January, practices are going to get even more intense. So eat right, do your daily stretching and workouts, and don't get soft. And for those of you going on ski trips"—she looks straight at me—"there will be no pulling, spraining, or breaking of any body parts. We need you. Understood?"

I smile. "Understood."

"Good. And there's one more thing. This is huge, so listen up, everyone. In some cultures, the start of a new year is the time where everyone who has wronged another person has to apologize before the Day of Repentance. Have any of you ever heard of that?"

I haven't, but a few other girls nod.

"All right," Coach says. "I'm implementing this concept. The deal is that there will not only be apologizing going on, but there will also be forgiving. I don't care why anyone is holding a grudge against anyone else on this team, but it's going to stop."

Ming rolls her eyes, just enough for me—and not Coach—to notice. I give a small shrug and sip my water.

Coach Laine looks around at all of us. "If you think I'm talking about you, I *am*. Get it together, ladies. Your last chance for repentance will be the first day back after the break. If you haven't found a way to make peace before practice that afternoon, you'll be running laps until your legs fall off and dancing in the back row for the rest of your high school careers. Hate to say it, but I'm not kidding. So get a little R and R—but not too much—keep in shape, and come back here in seventeen days as a team with one hundred percent unity, ready to work harder than you've ever worked before!"

All four of the team captains set down their water, push themselves off the floor, and clap and scream like cheerleaders. I can feel the stares of several of my teammates as they stand as well, but no matter what any of them might think, this Day of Repentance isn't my problem to solve.

I jump to my feet, pull Ming up, and cheer the loudest of everyone.

At the dinner table, I spoon my big brother's homemade salsa onto my tacos, while wanting more than anything to reach across the table to knock my little brothers' brown-haired heads together.

"It just doesn't add up," Zach says loudly. "I still don't believe it. I *refuse* to believe it."

"It happened," Jacob says even louder. "You saw it. Get over it."

"But Anakin wouldn't turn to the Dark Side of the Force. Not the way they showed it. I think they made a mistake."

"It doesn't matter what *you* think," says Jacob. "The people who made the movies got to decide. You can't change it."

Tony sets his margarita at the head of the table and takes his seat. "Sure he can. It's called 'fan fiction,' right?"

"Hey, guys?" Mom says, coming in from the kitchen. "I'm ready to enjoy a relaxing meal. Which means that effective immediately, two mouths are going to zip it about *Star Wars*. *Capisce?*"

Tony chuckles. "Which two? Because I'm interested in hearing Zach's ideas."

At the end of the table beside me, Bryan gives me a kill-me-now look from under his blond, bedhead hair. I push the salsa his way and hand him the spoon. Bryan and his girlfriend broke up right before the start of their winter break. He arrived home this week from college as the most depressed, making-all-of-our-lives-miserable version of himself imaginable.

Mom pulls out the empty chair between Emma and me. "I'm sure Zach has great thoughts, honey," she says to Tony as she sits, "and you can ask him all about it after dinner. Nicole, what time do you need to go to your sleepover tonight?"

Other than a few of my teachers, Mom is the only person who uses my real first name. She says that if she'd wanted to call me "Coley," that's what she would have put on my birth certificate.

"I'm fine for whenever you're ready to drop me off," I tell her. "I think everyone else who is going went straight after practice."

"Well, la-di-da," Jacob says.

I bite into my taco without responding. It isn't worth it.

"What happened to your neck?" Mom asks me.

I resist the urge to cover it as I finish chewing. "My curling iron fell out of my hand."

She leans in for a closer look. "Good grief. You need to put some burn gel on that. And when it scabs over, you better make sure not to pick at it or you'll give yourself a scar."

"Mom, I'm not going to pick at it."

"Let me see, Coley," Emma says.

"Why?"

She gives a big shrug and her blond curls bounce.

I lean in and tilt my head to expose the side of my neck for a couple of seconds—it's easier than making a thing out of it—but I can't bring myself to look anywhere except at my plate while I'm doing so.

"Does it hurt?" Emma asks.

"I can't even feel it."

"Yuck," Zach says. "I bet that burn's going to turn all blistered and super pus-y."

"Yuck," Jacob says. "Zach said, 'super pussy.'"

Emma laughs.

"I said, '*pus*-y!'" says Zach.

Mom scoops refried beans onto her plate. "Watch your mouths, all of you."

"I can't," Jacob says, pulling on his lips. "My mouth isn't big enough."

"Guess what, everyone," Tony cuts in. "I picked up the boards and skis from the shop today. They're all tuned up, waxed, and ready."

"Yes!" Jacob pumps his arm. "I'm gonna go on so many jumps this time."

I've been thinking all day about how to tell Mom and Tony about Reece joining us in a way that won't make them mad. I wish I could just *not* tell them until he shows up at the vacation house, but that would make it awkward for everyone—especially Reece. Anyway, his mom could call here at any time, so I have to get it over with.

I take a deep breath, let it out slowly, and then smile big, hoping my enthusiasm will be contagious. "Oh, hey. I wanted to tell you all. I found out that one of my friends is going to meet us up at Whistler for the last couple days of our trip. So that will be fun, right?"

"Which friend?" Mom asks. "Alejandra, I hope."

"No," I say, still smiling, even though, seriously, when is she going to accept that Alejandra and I don't go anywhere together anymore? "It's Reece. You met him, remember? He's in the marching band, and I introduced you when you came to watch me dance at Homecoming halftime? He's in jazz band, too."

That last part was for Tony's benefit, since he also likes all that old music.

Mom shakes her head, frowning like she can't keep up. "Your friend is a boy named Reece?"

This is already going in exactly the direction I'd hoped it wouldn't. The corners of my lips are threatening to slip downward. "Yes. He loves to snowboard. He'll drive himself up the day after Christmas, and it'll be great."

Tony raises his eyebrows. He and Mom exchange a long look, and then Tony says, "That kid doesn't think he's going to be staying with us, does he?"

"Where else would he stay?"

Mom rubs her temples. "Nicole, you can't invite a random boy to our town house whom we met once at a football game and you know that. Plus, we're so rarely all together these days. I'm sorry, but I think it will be better if this trip is for the family only."

My excited approach didn't work, so I have to switch tactics. "It's for *one* night. You were going to let Bryan bring Heather for the whole trip, and when you think about it, you hardly knew her, either."

Bryan shoots me a how-could-you-say-that-name-in-front-of-me look. I feel kind of bad about it, but I have to use any and all ammunition.

"Your brother happens to be twenty years old," Mom says. "Not fifteen."

"I'll be sixteen next month. Anyway, Reece is looking forward to this. It would be really mean to tell him he can't come now."

Tony shakes his head. "You should have thought about that before you invited him without permission. Besides, I can guess what that kid has on his mind and it isn't snowboarding."

Whenever Mom and Tony talk about What's on Boys' Minds, I want to scream.

"Is Reece the guy with the blue truck?" Zach asks.

"Yes," I say. "He's very, very nice and does a lot of favors for me."

"Oh, him," Jacob says. "He always stares at your butt when he drops you off."

"Jacob!" Mom says.

"He does! When she's walking away, he watches her—"

"That's enough," Mom interrupts.

I want to go off on Jacob, but I need to be calm and rational now. "Reece's mom is planning to call you soon. And I can have Reece come over so you can talk to him in person, too, if you want. You'll see that there's nothing to worry about."

"I don't know," Mom says.

I can tell that she's totally wavering, though. Just a little more convincing and she'll agree. "*Please*, Mom," I say.

Bryan slams his hand on the table. "Mom, what the hell? Why are you forcing her to beg? Quit making a big deal out of it and just let the guy come."

"Can you please not speak to your mother like that?" Tony says, tightening his jaw.

Mom sighs. "We didn't let you bring girls on vacation when you were your sister's age. It's not appropriate."

"What do you think could possibly happen?" Bryan asks. "We're *all* going to fucking be there."

Then, without another word, he stomps out of the room.

Mom pushes her chair back as if she's going to go after him, but she stops just as quickly and scoots back in. Tony gulps his drink while Emma, Jacob, and Zach stare at one another. I take another bite.

Bryan and I have been on the same team forever and ever: Us versus All of Them. When he's like this, though, it doesn't do me any good at all.

CHAPTER 4

Half an hour later, Mom drives me to the sleepover in silence. She isn't not speaking to me in an angry way; she's just lost in her own thoughts. I want to ask if she's made up her mind about Reece—if she's at least willing to think about it—but I know her well enough to wait this out.

We pull up in front of Piper and Noah's house. It's only a few blocks away, but Mom is paranoid and doesn't like me walking anywhere after dark. She puts the minivan in park and leaves the engine idling while I reach back and pull my stuff from the seat behind me.

"All right, he can come," she announces.

I don't pretend this hasn't been on my mind or start a new argument with her by asking "Who?" or "Where?" or, above all, "Why?" I just say, "Thank you."

The darkness and streetlights make her face glowy and shadowy at the same time and her dark brown eyes—which all five of us kids inherited—look almost black. "I have to tell you, though," she says, "it disappoints me that with you and Bryan, it's always everyone else who comes first. The rest of us would love to have time with you too, sometimes."

I hate it when she acts like we're some kind of Brady Bunch. We aren't two families who came together to form one big, happy family. Instead, when I was five and Bryan was nine, Mom moved us here to where she'd grown up in Washington State, divorced our father, married Tony, and had three children with him in one shot. Bryan and I were half of her original family; now we're the leftovers.

Mom pushes a blond curl behind her ear. "And truthfully, I wish you wouldn't let your brother influence you so much when he's home. Especially concerning Tony. He's a good dad and he doesn't deserve the attitudes."

Before I can stop myself, I mutter, "He isn't our dad."

"But he wants to be. He *tries*. I know you don't even remember living in New Zealand, but believe me, Nicole, we are a million times better off now than we were with Patrick."

She's right that I have no recollection of our lives before, but she's wrong about Tony trying so hard. His own kids come first with him. They always have and always will. "I guess I should go," I say, gesturing toward the house.

"Say hi to everyone for me."

"I will."

I carry my purple overnight case and matching sleeping bag across the sidewalk, and let myself in. My family has been close with the Crownes for almost as long as I can remember. Mr. Crowne and Tony are law firm partners, Mrs. Crowne and my mom are good friends, Piper has had a hopeless crush on Bryan for years, and, of course, Noah and I hang out all the time.

In the front room, rolled-up sleeping bags and backpacks are piled up all over, and I can hear voices, laughter, and music coming from farther back in the house. I set my things down and make my way to the living room. Tonight is pretty much guaranteed to be a typical Piper party where we'll all sit around talking, and nothing even remotely wild will happen if she has anything to say about it.

"Hey, everyone!" I call out over the music as I breeze into the room.

About half the girls from our team are here, lounging on couches, chairs, and the floor. They turn to look up at me, and in that instant, their faces become a blurry background for the stare that my former best friend is aiming my way.

Alejandra's here. She's on that chair right in front of me, even though Piper specifically told me that she wasn't invited. At least, I thought that's what she'd said.

I was *sure* of it.

I look away quickly. From the sofa, Piper's eyes meet mine. "I'm so glad you're finally here, Coley," she says, standing to give me a quick hug.

"Me too," I say, but I'm too busy trying to figure out what's happening to put any feeling into my words.

Behind Piper, Ming is chewing her pinky nail and frowning at her lap.

"What'd I miss?" I ask, trying to ignore the knot in my stomach. "Not the ice cream, I hope."

Piper shakes her head. "Not at all. But there's something we need to talk about first."

She leads me to squish onto the couch between her and Ming, grabs the remote from the coffee table, and turns down the music.

I glance around at Dia, Olivia, Rachel B., Liz, Becca, Megan, Felicia, Rachel S., and Hannah. No one is talking and their expressions give nothing away, but I have a feeling that I know what's coming.

"We all heard what Coach Laine said at practice about the Day of Repentance," Piper says, using her squad-captain voice again. "Now, Coley. Alejandra. We all know you haven't been getting along. Coach wants you to work it out because your rift is affecting everyone. That's why I invited you both here tonight."

Just like I thought—a surprise intervention. This might end up being my least favorite Piper party ever.

I put on a big smile. "We won the competition last week, and we're going to keep winning. So I guess I don't know what the problem is."

"The problem," Felicia says, sitting up straighter in her chair, "is that I spend more time with this team than I do with anyone, and the nonstop tension is getting so old."

Hannah nods from her spot on the floor. "And it isn't Alejandra's fault. Maybe if some people were a little more supportive—"

"Oh, please!" Ming interrupts. "It isn't like Coley hasn't been trying to make things better. She even stopped changing in the locker room so that Alejandra can have her space—"

"More like so that she can keep avoiding Alejandra," Liz says.

As someone who has helped smooth over arguments between my teammates many times, I'm so not used to having all this hostility directed at me.

Piper puts her hand up like a crossing guard. "Stop, please. Don't make it worse. Let's all go put together our sundaes so that Coley and Alejandra can talk alone."

Everyone gets up slowly to leave the room. Hannah and Liz glare at me as they head to the kitchen. Dia pats my shoulder, while Ming quietly says, "I didn't have anything to do with this."

"I know," I tell her. Ming would never set me up. Not in the way that Piper obviously would. "Save me some marshmallow sauce, okay?"

Then it's just Alejandra and me.

All I want to do is sprint from the room. There's nowhere to go, though, and dealing with her is still preferable to sleeping in my own bed tonight. I sink farther into the couch cushions, bracing myself.

"Just so you know," Alejandra says, "they sprang it on me, too. Piper told me you weren't coming."

"I figured."

She scoots forward in her chair. "But since we're both here, we should try to talk. Don't you think?"

I study the throw pillow next to my elbow, and run my fingers through the beige fringe. "Why?"

"Because we need to."

"Why?"

"Because it's important."

"Why?"

I know that I sound like my brother Jacob, but I don't know how else to respond to her. With anyone else, I might be able to fake my way through this. Not with her, though. Never with her.

"Because," she says through her teeth. "Coach wants us to work this out and so does everyone else."

I remain silent. I don't look up.

Alejandra continues. "What is your problem? We did everything together from the beginning of sixth grade until two months ago. Now you're acting like the past four years don't matter, like it's all just *whatever* to you."

It's been longer than two months since she got together with the guy we both liked and started ditching me for him all the time—more like five months, actually—but I don't bother correcting her. "Of course it matters," I say.

I mean it too. Being around her right now makes me too uncomfortable, too angry, too exhausted, too much of too many things to be "whatever."

She gets up from her chair and stares down at me, making it impossible for me to keep from looking at her. "Okay," she says. "Then why are you being like this?"

"Like what?"

"Like, an unbelievable bitch!" She practically spits her words at me. "You said you were fine with me going out with Derrick. Now it's like you want to get revenge on me because he picked me instead of you. Neither of us has him now, so why don't you get over your jealousy and stop holding this stupid grudge?"

At that, I'm on my feet too, and Alejandra's eyes widen. We're at opposite sides of the coffee table, poised as if we're getting ready to jump into the middle of a boxing ring. "Guess what, Alejandra! I don't care about being with Derrick and I'm not dying of jealousy. So why don't *you* get over your delusions already?"

It's been a long time since we've really looked each other in the eye. What I want most is to turn away from her angry gaze, but I somehow manage to hold strong, all while standing composed with my posture perfect.

"I don't understand you," she says, crossing her arms over her chest. "I swear, you have got to be the most self-centered person and the worst friend in the world."

"Whatever," I say with a shrug.

I'm trying not to seem upset. I'm trying not to mope around. But after two hours, Alejandra's words are still distracting me from the laid-back-Piper-party fun that I should be having.

An Unbelievable Bitch.

The Most Self-Centered Person.

The Worst Friend in the World.

I can't believe she said those things to me. After all the times that I listened and tried to help with any and all of her issues. All the times that I dropped whatever I was doing just because she asked me to. All the times I kept my own problems to myself even though what I really wanted was for my best friend to notice *just once* that I don't have it all together either. And now she's saying this ridiculous stuff about Derrick. I mean, yeah, I liked him. Alejandra and I met him in eighth grade at the performing arts camp we go to every summer for the dance program. He's into acting and it was always fun to gush together over his hotness and joke about all the things we'd do with him if we ever got the chance.

But then this past July, she did get the chance. It stung that Derrick wanted her to be his girlfriend instead of me, but I got over it. What I can't get over is that she broke up with him on their three-month anniversary and blamed it on me.

A loud, male voice jolts me from my thoughts. "I knew it. I totally called this!"

I glance up from my *InStyle* magazine and watch Noah strut into the front room carrying a bottle of clear alcohol. His parents went to bed, but if Piper sees that in his hand, she's going to go crazy.

Noah settles on the floor next to my sleeping bag. "I saw the stack of movies out earlier and said, 'No way is Coley going to make it through a horror flick.' And now everyone's in there watching it and you're here hiding like I knew you would be."

Not *everyone's* in there. Alejandra stomped out after our

argument, and Hannah and Liz took off with her. Our team—especially Piper's squad—is even more divided than before.

"I'm not hiding," I say to Noah.

"Right," he says with a grin. "So, you've suddenly stopped crying and running away from scary movies, then?"

"Ha-ha."

Noah has an annoying way of constantly bringing up embarrassing things that I wish he would forget already. The truth is, it doesn't matter much what they're watching; I'm avoiding Piper and her disappointment in me as much as I am the movie.

"Listen," Noah says. "You're not the only one. I got so freaked out when my dad took me to one of those *Saw* movies that I pissed my pants. *In* the theater."

"Gross, Noah."

"The good news is that I can help you. Do you want to know how?"

I do, but I don't want to flat-out admit that he's right in thinking that I still have nightmares even though I'm almost sixteen. "You want to tell me how you recovered from the disgustingness of peeing yourself in public?"

"There's no getting over that," he says. "But getting over the patheticness of being afraid was easy. I just decided not to let it get to me anymore. I reminded myself that the actors were playing roles and that lots of people were working behind the scenes. You know, special effects and makeup and music and everything. Everyone involved in creating those movies was trying to scare me and I refused to give them the satisfaction."

I manage a small smile. "You sure showed them."

"*Yeah*, I did. And you can too!"

He raises his arm and we high-five. I let my hand drop on top of my sleeping bag, and he takes it in his. It isn't in any way romantic. It truly never has been, even though Noah and I have gone to all of the school dances together since we were twelve, and he seems totally fine with everyone at school thinking that we're together.

I've secretly been suspicious for a long time that there isn't any girl in the world who will ever have a chance with him. I saw some pictures on his computer last year of guys kissing and stuff. Add to that the fact that Kimber snuck into his room and tried to make out with him two weeks ago, and he—according to Ming—walked out and slept in the garage, and it proves to me that I'm right.

"By the way," Noah says, letting my hand go and leaning against the couch. "Reece Kinsey's still trying to make me hate you. He was talking about you in pre-calc. The. Whole. Fricken. Class period."

I feel myself blushing. I kind of wish that Reece wouldn't

talk about me. And yet . . . I kind of like that he does.

Noah goes on. "Last week, I had to listen to him complain for *days* about his mom and dad being cock blockers about your ski trip. I told him to just kill the visiting grandparents and solve his problem for good. It didn't go over well, though."

"No?"

"No. It seems that his sense of humor is broken, at least in regards to the Amazing Coley Sterling. He worships you. I'm not even kidding."

And now I'm back to wishing Reece wouldn't discuss me—at least not with Noah. "I don't want to be worshipped."

"Then Reece isn't the guy for you."

His words hit me harder than they should, but I try not to show it.

Noah lifts the bottle. "Truth, dare, or drink?"

"Oh, you know me," I say, with a wave. "I'm not the daring type and I totally hate telling the truth."

He nods. "I hear you. Drink it is then."

I glance over my shoulder. "Piper will get mad at me, you know. *More* mad, I should say."

Noah doesn't look surprised or ask me what happened, which makes me wonder if he already knows.

He and Alejandra were never close, but they were both my friends, so they hung out sometimes. In the weeks after

Alejandra and I stopped speaking, Noah tried to get information out of me, but I made it clear that I wasn't going to talk about it. He stopped trying.

"Do we really care that my sister's a"—Noah makes an imaginary box in the air in front of him—"square?"

Honestly, I care a lot, but right now I want Noah to stay with me more. I motion like I'm drawing a cartoon speech bubble out of my mouth and over my head. "Insert more weak protests here."

And then we drink.

CHAPTER 5

It's almost midnight two nights later and Ming and I are perched in the dark on her bedroom windowsill, preparing to make our escape.

"You first?" she asks.

"No, *you*." I move aside. "Show me how it's done."

It isn't an incredibly long way down—Ming's room is on the ground floor—but there are tons of bushes below. She dangles her legs, pushes off from the side of the house, catches her foot on a crispy-looking hydrangea, and falls to her hands and knees on a pile of dead leaves.

Holding in a laugh, I whisper down to her, "That was graceful. Are you okay?"

"Fine, fine," she says, hopping up and brushing her palms over the front of her jeans.

I check that my backpack is securely on my shoulders

and then make the same jump—except I manage to miss the vicious plants and land on my feet.

Ming sticks out her tongue. "Show off."

She pushes her way back to the window, reaches up, and inches it across its track until it's almost closed.

I zip my coat to my chin. We're both wearing lots of layers like Xander suggested, but I'm still feeling the chill. My breath steams in front of me as I dig my gloves out of my pockets and pull them on.

"All right," Ming says. "Let's go!"

We creep out of the yard, and then when we're about a block away, we start skipping down the sidewalk like hyper kids at recess. It's eerily quiet in her housing development, and I'm wound up; I *finally* get to see Reece for the first time since Christmas break started two days ago. All I want to do is jump around and dance, dance, dance.

"Did Xander tell you where we're going yet?" I ask.

"All he'd say is that they're picking us up at the park. My guess is that after that we'll probably end up at some abandoned boxcar or secret cave somewhere. You know how my boyfriend is."

"Horny?" I've seen them all over each other enough times— totally against my will, obviously—to know that that's the truth of it.

Ming gives me a push. "I meant that he's *adventurous*. Anyway, I'll make sure that wherever we end up, you and you-know-who get some quality alone time."

"Well, okay!" I laugh like she's beyond strange for bringing it up. I'm looking forward to exchanging Christmas presents with Reece, but the idea of "quality time" is kind of outside my comfort zone.

We turn the corner and reach the park. The parking lot is empty, so we make our way across the grass. "I can't stop wondering why you're so weird about him," Ming says in a way-too-concerned sounding voice as we approach the swings.

"I'm not."

"You *are*." She's still being serious. "You won't even admit to liking him. He's going on vacation with your family. You're together all the time. You got him a stuffed giraffe for Christmas. It doesn't get any more obvious, but you still won't confess to me!"

I reach back and pat my bag containing Reece's gift. The first time I ever really talked to him was earlier in the fall at the zoo after Ming and Xander disappeared on us. Reece and I then paid extra for the chance to hand-feed bamboo leaves to the giraffes, and immediately afterward, I tripped and took him down to the ground with me. It was embarrassing, but he was nice about the whole thing and we've been hanging out ever since.

"It's a stupid present to get for a boy, isn't it?" I ask Ming.

"No, it's very cute." She sits on a swing. "And if there was ever a boy who's exactly the right amount of sappy to appreciate it, it's Reece."

The frowny-faced way she's looking at me makes my chest tighten. Alejandra was my best friend for so long that I was used to sharing most of my secrets with only her. The fact that we're not close anymore is an understatement, but maybe I can have something like that with Ming.

"All right," I blurt out. "I like him."

That's all it takes for Ming's lips and cheeks to spring into a positively gleeful expression. "You like *who*?"

I kick the wood chips at my feet. "Who do you think?"

"Oh, no. You're not getting off the hook, Coley. Say it!"

There's no reason why this should be hard. Four words. I've spoken all of them before—just never in this particular order. I take a deep breath, let it out slowly. "I like . . . Reece Kinsey."

Ming makes a high-pitched squeal and jumps up. "You *like* him like him?"

"Yes!"

"The kind of like where you want to rev his engine or actually use his gearshift?"

I burst out laughing. Leave it to her to be completely unromantic. "I don't know. Maybe both someday?"

She shrieks and throws her arms around me. We hug and hop up and down, and I'm glad that I played along because this is a lot like what it used to feel like when I had a best friend.

"He's good for you, you know," Ming says, going back to her swing. "I mean, he's a little geeky and all, but you're so cute together."

I get on the swing next to hers. "Reece went out with Violet for a long time, right?"

"I think for, like, two years."

"He never talks about her. Not with me, at least. Is that weird?"

"Of course not! She's in college now and they are completely over and done with."

I've never had a boyfriend, but it's weird to me that people can be important to each other for two years and then just *not* be anymore. "Do you think it's true what people say about them?" I ask.

"You mean that they got it on over four hundred times?"

"Um!" I pump my legs to get some air, wishing, wishing, wishing she hadn't told me that. My question was going to be about whether they'd *for sure* for sure hooked up; I'd never heard this crazy number before. "Is that even possible?" I ask. "That many times in two years?"

"*Wellll*," Ming says. "From what I've heard, Reece and Violet had exactly two things in common. And they both happened to begin with *s* and end with *x*."

I take a moment to work it out. Sex, obviously. *Obviously.*

Four! Hundred! Times!

And the second thing? Oh, right. Sax. Violet was in band too.

"Aww, Coley." Ming leans toward me a little as we sail through the air, completely out of sync. "You don't have to worry. Reece is way over that nympho and totally into you. I promise."

"I'm not worried," I say, forcing a smile. "It's just that I haven't even been kissed four hundred times."

"Oh, I don't know. You probably have, actually. I hear that kisses add up fast when you're, you know, naked with someone."

Like most of the rest of our team, Ming's heard my Truth or Dare confessions: Noah was my experimental first kiss when I was fourteen, and I came very close to going all the way with a guy named Pedro whom I met at a wedding reception a couple of months later. What no one knows—not even Alejandra—is that both of those stories are complete lies.

Has Reece heard these things about me? Does he think that I'm like Violet? *Am* I like her, and I don't even know it yet?

As if she's reading my mind, Ming says, "Reece sure does have a type, doesn't he?"

"He does?" I yelp.

"Short, tiny blondes with huge chests."

"What? My chest isn't that huge!"

She laughs. "Not like Violet's. That's still three out of four. You're way, way, way prettier than her, though."

"Why, thank you!"

"Why, you're welcome."

A familiar blue truck pulls into the parking lot just then. Ming jumps out of her swing and turns to grin with triumph after landing without even a stumble. "Here they are!" she sings.

And here we go.

When Ming and I get to Reece's truck, she yanks the passenger door open and barrels into Xander, giving him the loudest, longest kiss imaginable. As they climb into the back on the jump seats and start kissing again, I glance at Reece. He's smiling his just-for-me smile and I freeze.

"Are you . . . getting in?" he asks.

I'm not going to picture him with his ex-girlfriend. I'm not going to think about their two years as a couple, or their *four hundred* times together. I'm not going to stand here worrying and wondering if he wants that from me, too.

No, no, no, no, no.

No!

"As a matter of fact, I *am* getting in," I say, returning his smile.

I strap on my seat belt, and Reece takes off. It's obvious that, for some reason, he gelled his usually light-brown hair tonight, making it look dark and stiff. It doesn't quite work for him, but it doesn't totally *not* work, either. I don't know what it is, but his dorky fashion missteps win me over every time.

In the back, Ming and Xander finally break apart—it's easy to tell even without looking since the way they kiss sounds like they're slurping from cereal bowls—and I turn toward Xander. "So, where are we going?"

"This girl," Xander says, shaking his head at Ming. The "rock star" hair he's been growing out is covering his eyes, and he pushes it back. "How many times do we have to go over this? It's called a 'surprise' because you don't get to know before we get there."

"Just go with it," Ming says with a smile in her voice as she pokes my arm.

"Coley needs to learn to be true to her roots," Xander says. "Australians are supposed to be all about adventure."

"She doesn't have Australian roots," says Reece. "She's a half Kiwi from New Zealand."

"Half Kiwi, half strawberry?" Xander asks.

Xander happens to be the person in this truck who's technically known me the longest, and who also knows me the least. He's a grade ahead of me—just like Reece and Ming—and we never hung out until he got together with Ming before Homecoming. The main thing I know about him is that he's as music obsessed as Reece: He plays drums for the marching band and is also in a band with some guys from school.

"I'm half Kiwi, half American," I tell him.

"I spent the night at Coley's last night," Ming says. "So I got to meet her older brother and hear his cool accent. Which made me wonder—why don't you have an accent, Coley?"

"Why do you think?" I ask. "We moved here when I was little and I've been surrounded by you people ever since."

I don't tell them the rest—that Bryan pretty much lost his accent too, until it magically reappeared when he got to high school. As far as I know, no one has called him out for it, but it seems to me that he does it to impress girls. Case in point: He sounded *almost* like a regular West Coast American all week until Ming came over yesterday.

"You can't blame me," Ming says. "I've only known you since last year."

"Me too," Reece says.

Ming moved here from Oregon at the start of my ninth-grade year and Reece moved here from Alaska the year before that when I was still in middle school.

There's silence for a moment, and then Xander says, "Okay. I admit it. It was all me. When I was in second grade and Coley was in first, I enlisted everyone in the country to help me make her lose her accent. Television, movies, day-to-day conversations. We were ruthless."

"This is what happens when Xander puts his mind to something," Reece says.

"Looking back, it was a pretty huge success," Xander deadpans. "Especially when you consider that my power of persuasion these days is twenty percent effective at best."

"No way." Ming gives him another loud kiss. "It's more like forty-five."

The kissing continues and I keep my eyes directed straight ahead. "So, Reece!" I practically yell so that I can drown out the smacking sounds. "I see that you've brought us to the Valley. Are we going to the river? The railroad tracks? A tattoo shop? I wouldn't mind stopping for a snack somewhere!"

"How does the highway leading out of town sound?" Reece asks, raising his voice extra-loud too.

"Only if we can drop off these two!"

"You might as well give up the guessing game now," Xander says to us. "You won't be able to figure out where I'm taking you because I guarantee that you've never been there. Oh, and you need to take a right there past the school." After directing Reece through a few more turns, Xander says, "Okay, slow down. The driveway we want is hidden, but there's a 'For Sale' sign kind of sticking out of some bushes. See it? There!"

The truck bounces us down a long gravel driveway between thick trees until we reach a clearing. Reece parks in front of an imposing building.

"Hey, I've been here before," I tell them.

"No!" Xander says.

"Yes! I've come here tons of times. Just never from that direction."

Everyone laughs, obviously thinking I made it up to mess with Xander. We pile out of the truck and they all stare up at the structure. It was going to be a house at one time, but it was never finished. It has no siding or doors, and someone nailed black plastic over where the windows should be. Alejandra once told me that she heard the builder ran out of money.

"Awesome, right?" Xander asks, switching on a flashlight.

"Yes," Ming says, kind of breathlessly as she takes his free hand. "And the sky tonight is like stars piled on top of stars."

Reece raises an eyebrow and I bite back a laugh.

"Are you going to show us how to get inside?" Reece asks me, teasingly.

"*I* can show you," Xander says. "I've actually been here before, remember?"

He and Ming head toward the house, Reece follows, and I bring up the rear. I hope none of them ever tell anyone else about this place; I'd hate for partiers to come in and trash it.

Xander pulls on a sheet of plywood that's attached with a hinge. It creaks open like a human-sized cupboard door. He and Ming rush inside, taking the flashlight and its glow with them.

"Jeez," Reece says, "it would have been nice if he'd clued us in about the need for flashlights, maybe."

I pull out my phone. "Pretty sure I already have one."

"Ah, good thinking," he says, taking his out too.

We press buttons for about two minutes and then make our way carefully through what would have been a garage, past dozens of wooden beams, and up the stairs, shining our phones at our feet. My eyes were pretty well adjusted outside, but it's completely black in here and I can't see more than three steps ahead of me.

When we get up on the second floor, Reece lifts his phone up high and a soft glow illuminates the framed rooms without walls. "It *is* pretty cool," he says. "It'll be a nice house if some-one finishes it."

"Me!" I say. "Ever since I was thirteen, it's been my secret wish to buy it someday."

"So you really have been here?"

"Alejandra lives down the street and this was our hideout. Back, you know, before we stopped being friends."

He nods slowly as if he's waiting for more.

I don't know what to say, though—we never talk about her—so I change the subject. "It's set up for five bedrooms and four bathrooms. That's where a bathroom would be, obvi-ously." I point toward a tub. "And over there's the kitchen. And then the dining room."

"So this must be the living room?"

"Yes. And that's the master suite. There's also two bed-rooms downstairs and the other two are on the third floor. It's actually really cool up there. We stashed sleeping bags and games and flashlights. I'll show you."

I make my way up the next flight of stairs with Reece on my heels, hoping Alejandra hasn't taken the stuff out in the months since I've been here.

When we're almost to the top, Reece takes my arm gently. "Um. Given the sound effects," he whispers up to me, "I don't think we want to keep going."

He's right. I cover my mouth to hold in my giggles as we tiptoe back down.

"One of these days we'll learn, right?" I say, when we're safely on the second floor.

"Yeah, one of these days." He takes a seat on the steps and pats his hand on floor beside him, so I sit too. "I don't know why they keep bringing us. I'm going to pretend that they're eating soup up there."

We're so close that our elbows are touching. I can just barely feel it through all my layers. "Ooh. Chicken and stars?" I ask. "That's my favorite."

"I was thinking more like the noodley kind you have to slurp. And actually, soup sounds really good right about now. Just not, you know, *their* soup."

I laugh. "Now that you said that, I'm totally hungry. It sucks that restaurants are closed this late."

"Not being able to suck soup sucks." Reece shakes his fist in the direction of the upper staircase and calls out, "Damn you, Xander and Ming!"

I giggle again and he joins in.

Maybe it's weird, but I kind of wonder what they're doing. Ming is a total "Dare" girl—she's never picked Truth when I've been around—so all I know is what I've seen. Which happens to have been Ming and Xander kissing pretty much nonstop when they're hanging out with Reece and me.

"So you're heading out in the morning?" Reece asks.

"Late morning. We can't check into the town house until four."

My shoulder bumps his arm. I leave it there and he doesn't pull away.

"And I'm going to be stuck doing holiday and tourist stuff with my parents and grandparents for six days straight," he says. "The curse of being an only child."

"Believe me, you won't think it's a curse anymore after staying with my family. You'll be dying to escape to your own life."

"We'll see," he says.

Our faces are close. He's smiling at me and I'm smiling back. I wish I didn't have my gloves on because he's shifted his hand so that it's kind of touching mine.

"Have I ever told you," I say, "that I'm going to miss you like the deserts miss the rain?"

"Nope. But the song is by Everything But the Girl."

"Gah!" I playfully slug his shoulder. "You're too good at this. Your brain is like a music encyclopedia."

"Not really," he says. "I looked it up after we heard it the other day."

"Me too, actually."

I'm constantly researching songs these days, trying to find good lyrics to use for this silly game of ours.

Reece says, "Have I ever told you that I'll miss you like a child misses their blanket?"

"Fergie?" I suggest. "Or the Black Eyed Peas?"

"That would be Fergie."

"I thought so. And by the way, my compliment was better than yours. I mean, a *blanket*?"

He shrugs, still smiling. "Was yours really a compliment, though? Lack of rain. That's what makes a desert a desert. So adding rain would turn it into something else. Would a desert even want that?"

"Yes! It's a known fact that all deserts secretly aspire to become jungles because jungles have waterfalls and pretty plants and flowers."

"All right," he says, with a crooked little smile. "But just so you know, I happen to think blankets are awesome. Especially, you know, those really soft ones? Man, would I miss a blanket like that."

My heart dances in double time. "Would you really?"

"I would." He glances in the direction of the third floor. "So, um. Your Christmas present. It's in my truck."

"Which is the same place yours is."

He helps me up and doesn't let go of my hand. I can hardly

breathe as the light from his phone guides us down the stairs. Something's going to happen. I think so, at least.

I hope so.

We're sitting beside each other on Reece's bucket seats. I yank off my gloves and unzip my coat partway while Reece starts the engine for some heat and turns on the light overhead.

"Ouch," he says. "What happened to your neck? Wait. Don't tell me. Vampire bite?"

"Actually, curling iron burn. It's very attractive, I know."

It's very painful, too. I accidentally ripped the burned layer of skin off today while I was drying myself after my shower. Mom taped a gel pad over the open wound, which makes it look worse than it is, but eases the throbbing somewhat.

Reece pulls a small rectangular package from under his seat and gives it to me. "Hope you don't hate it."

"I'm not going to hate it."

Even though I have no guesses whatsoever about what it might be, it's from Reece so it's going to be perfect. I know it.

I rip into the silver snowflake paper and find . . . a box of granola bars.

"Peanut butter chocolate chip!" I say, making a big deal out of holding it up high so that he won't realize how disappointed I am.

He's watching me, grinning probably even bigger than I am. "You eat those every day after dancing, right?"

I nod. "Uh-huh!"

"Cool. I thought so."

"Well. Yeah. Thank you. So much!"

"You're welcome."

He looks from my face to the box and back again like he wants me to tear it open and eat one right now. I hand him the smashed gift bag that I brought for him, and while he's sliding his hand into the tissue paper, I drop the box he gave me into my backpack.

Granola bars. Reece got me *granola bars* for Christmas.

He pulls out the stuffed giraffe and a huge smile spreads across his face. "Oh, wow. Coley, this is so awesome. You have no idea."

He seems to mean it, but maybe he's a liar like me. Maybe we're both terrible gift-givers and way-too-polite receivers of terrible gifts.

"Are you sure?" I ask. "Is a stuffed animal for a boy weird?"

He shakes his head. "No way. She's cool. And soft. Like a blanket. You know, the kind of blanket that I would miss."

I burst out laughing at that.

And now it's time for me to get over it. Because, okay, he did give me a totally not-great present, but he made sure it was something that I'd like, at least. It's really sweet the way he pays attention to things like that.

Reece sets the giraffe on his lap. "I'll name her after you. Your middle name's Marie?"

I nod. He must know that from when I showed him my driving permit a few weeks ago.

He stares down at the giraffe. "No, not a Marie," he muses. "She's a Sterling. Now the big question: Sleeping with her—creepy or cute?"

"Hmm." I rub my chin, pretending to consider. "Definitely cute."

"Cool." He slouches way, way down, and sits with his body turned slightly toward me and the side of his face pressed against his seat. "That was a good day, wasn't it? With the giraffes?"

"Of course it was." I ease into that same position, facing him. "We fed them, I knocked you on the ground, giving us both bruises all over our bodies, and then we ate ice cream. Best day ever!"

"Best day ever, *so far*," he says. "I've always thought that maybe you meant to fall on me. Because, I mean, the way you walk. And dance. You're so graceful. For you to accidentally trip and take me down with you. It doesn't seem possible."

He's staring into my eyes and I'm getting totally lost. "I promise you," I say softly, "it was very possible and very accidental. There should be a law against cracks in sidewalks like that."

He brushes my hair back from my cheek and my heart kicks into quadruple time.

Oh my God, oh my God.

"Well, see," he says. "I was kind of hoping you'd done it on purpose."

"Oh. Then the next time I take you down it will be."

"Okay," he says, nodding.

I nod too. We're watching each other and our heads keep moving and moving and I'm getting dizzier and dizzier and I wish that he would just lean in and kiss me or that I had the guts to lean in and kiss him but he *isn't* and I *don't* but I want to, I really, really want to, and I'm going to make myself sick if I don't stop nodding—

Reece's door flies open and we jump back from each other.

"Hooray!" Ming grabs Sterling from Reece and makes her dance all over the steering wheel, completely not seeming to notice that she just interrupted what was supposed to be our "quality time."

"See what Coley got for Reece?" she says to Xander. "Isn't she cuuuute?"

Reece is still looking at me. "I think she's beautiful."

CHAPTER 6

It's the day of our trip and every single person in my family is stressing me out. Mom's panicking because, like usual, she waited until the last possible second to pack her clothes. Tony keeps yelling at us kids to help load the vehicles so that we can "get on the road already!" Bryan's stomping around and muttering to himself about "this goddamned family" while Jacob, Emma, and Zach battle fiercely over who's sitting where and which movies they should watch during the drive.

The only things keeping me from losing my mind are texts with my friends.

> *Ming: I'm soooo sorry about last nite. The engine was running - we thought you were leaving! You forgive me, rite?*
>
> *Me: I suppose I forgive you ;)*

Dia: Have fun in Canada! We should all do something after you get back!

Me: We should!

Reece: Au revoir

Me: Adios!

Reece: Sawatdi (I looked that up. It's Thai)

Me: Nomistay! (from my yoga video. I probably spelled it wrong)

"Coley!" Tony yells over his shoulder on his way out the door. "Please put your phone away and tell your mother we're about to leave without her! Let's go, kids. Outside."

They all file out.

"Hey, Mom!" I call.

She comes around the corner with her purse over her shoulder, dragging her suitcase behind her. "I heard. And I'm ready."

I shove my phone into my coat pocket, and Mom follows me. Outside, Tony has started up the minivan and the triplets are piling into it. Bryan is standing next to his car with the driver-side door open, staring at the ground. I wait at the top of the driveway, suddenly not sure where to go.

"Nicole, you're riding with Bryan?" Mom asks in a tone

suggesting that my answer had better be yes.

"I *can*," I say.

I glance at Bryan to try to gauge if it's what he wants, but he just climbs in and slams the door.

"Here's your permission letter," Mom says. "You have your passport?"

I nod and she wraps her arms around me. "Do something about your brother, okay?" she whispers, even though no one except me can hear her. "He needs you. You're the only one who can get through to him."

That used to be true. "I'll try."

She lets go and tucks my hair behind my ear. "What does Yoda say? 'Do it or do not do it. There's no such thing as try'?"

"Something like that."

I sit next to Bryan and before I've even closed my door, he shoves into reverse. Emma waves at me out her window and I wave back.

"What's Mom's deal?" Bryan asks.

"She gave me a travel permission letter for you to show the border guards. And botched a *Star Wars* quote."

He rolls his eyes and turns up the music—the same angry-sounding stuff that's been coming from his room all week. Louder and louder and louder. It's bass kicking my back through the seat. It's an awful voice screaming syllables instead of words. It's treble stabbing my brain.

We ride this way for over an hour. It's the total opposite of silence, but it feels even lonelier somehow. Every so often, I sneak glances at Bryan's profile. The skin all around his eyes is dark and puffy, his jaw and cheeks are stubbly, and his mouth is turned down. It's as if he's given up.

Noah: r u gonna bring me some nice Cubans from bc
Me: Sorry. I'm not spending 10 years in jail over illegal cigars for you :)
Noah: chicken id do it 4 u

Ming: I'm sure you'll be kissing in canada! . . . you still never told me what Reece gave you????
Me: Thats your punishment. You can never know! Mwha-haha

Reece: Nomaskaar (That's goodbye in Bengali. Looked this up too, in case you couldn't guess)
Me: See ya! (New Zealand)
Reece: LOL. Yadalanh (Apache for "farewell")

About twenty miles before the border, Bryan finally turns down the music. "Do you need me to stop?" he asks.

"I'll be fine for a while."

Out of the corner of my eye, I see him slide his hand into his shirt pocket and pull out a joint and a lighter. Fantastic.

It isn't like he doesn't know the deal. If you want to get in and out of Canada with as few issues as possible, you turn off your radio, remove your sunglasses and hat, and be extra-polite when answering the guards' questions—even if they happen to be in the mood to be stern toward you. You do *not* get stoned less than thirty minutes before trying to cross.

Bryan breathes in deeply and holds the joint out for me.

"I don't smoke," I say, staring straight ahead out the dirty, rain-splattered windshield. "And I have to tell you, I was really counting on not getting arrested at the border today."

"Jesus, Coley. Relax. I don't have any more on me. I'm not an idiot. Plus, everyone knows BC Bud is the best. I'll just buy it when I get there."

"You do that."

He opens his window a few inches and the wind blows his hair all around. He needs a haircut. "What's your problem?" he asks. "I drive better when I'm stoned. So what? And don't act like you're so above it. I've seen you smoke before."

This is one of the first official conversations between the two of us since he came home with Heather for a couple of weeks back in July, and wow, am I hating every second of it.

"*That* was a one-time, never-going-to-happen-again occurrence," I say.

"It was hilarious is what it was. You stared at my carpet, I swear, for an hour, like you'd never seen anything so awesome in your life."

I don't answer. We've never talked about it, never even admitted out loud that it happened. At the time, I was about to start ninth grade and Bryan was about to start his freshman year of college. I was upset because it was his last night home before he left for the University of Connecticut, so I decided to get high with him. He told me I needed to smoke a lot since it was my first time, so I took hit after hit until I lost count. Then I laughed, cried, pretty much lost the use of my limbs, and fell into a restless sleep filled with hallucinations. The truth is, I haven't gotten over it, I will never get over it, and the pungent smell of Bryan's weed now is threatening to take my mind to a place that I don't want it to go.

"I've been thinking about what you said to me that night," Bryan says in a more pleasant tone than before. "You know, after we talked about how I could have gone to school near home if Tony hadn't basically forced me to go to his old school?"

I wish he would *drop* this. "I don't remember anything that I said aside from your hair looking plastic like a Fisher-Price toy."

"You also told me, 'You don't have to do what Tony wants. We can run away. We don't need him or his money.'"

"And, obviously, I was high," I say.

"That's the thing, though. You were right. We don't need him. We don't need anyone. I mean, we have dual citizenship and could even go back to New Zealand if we wanted to."

"Sure. Let's do that, after Mom's moved us halfway around the world to get away from the man who threw her at walls and broke her ribs and arms."

"Okay, fine," he says, shrugging. "Not New Zealand then. But I'm just so over this, you know? Mom and Tony can have their perfect little family without us and we can take off. I'm ready to start over."

"Well, I'm not."

He stares at me, shocked. "It was your idea in the first place!"

"That was over a year ago. My big brother was moving across the country and I was about to start high school. It was scary. But you know what? I got through it and I don't hate my life. I'm on an awesome dance team. We made State last year and we're going to do it again this year. I have a lot of friends—"

"Like this Reece guy? Is that who you keep texting?"

I place my phone in the car door pocket. "Despite what Mom and Tony might have you believe, his name isn't 'This

Reece Guy' or 'That Reece Kid.' It's just Reece."

"All right. So is 'just Reece' your boyfriend or what?"

I don't want to talk about that, either. There's no way for me to know if Bryan's going to make fun of me or be all protective older brother-ish about it. I have no doubt that the only reason he defended me and told Mom that she should let Reece meet up with us is because it was the opposite of what she and Tony wanted.

"Why did you and Heather break up?" I ask, avoiding his question entirely.

Bryan groans. "Coley, come on."

"Just tell me. You bailed on us for Thanksgiving to be with *her* family. What happened between then and last week?"

"She's a bitch and I hate her," he says, running his hand roughly over his hair. "End of story."

"I'm sure she's always been that way, but that didn't keep you from forcing her on us during your vacations last year."

He glances my way, chewing his lip and narrowing his eyes like he's trying to process what I just said. Like he really had no idea all this time that I couldn't stand his girlfriend. Which, I guess, makes sense since it isn't like I was ever rude to her like she was to me.

"I thought she was the one, you know?" Bryan says. "And the thing that sucks the most is that she got to decide it was over and

I have to live with it. Do you have any idea what that's like?"

I shake my head, but in a way, I can relate. A little bit, maybe. It's kind of like when Bryan left last fall. He'd been there since I was born. He calmed me down whenever I had bad dreams, picked me up at Alejandra's after my dance lessons and his basketball practices, and was always, always on my side no matter what. Then he wasn't there for me anymore. And really, he hasn't been ever since.

He continues. "It took me off-guard. Totally knocked me on my ass. I mean, she broke up with me in a text, of all things."

I turn toward him. "What?"

"Yeah. She was late meeting me at the restaurant for my birthday. I texted, asking where she was, and she basically said she wasn't coming and it was over between us. And that was it. She won't talk to me. She won't see me." His voice cracks. "She changed her profile online to 'single' and put up a picture of her kissing some dude that I don't even know."

"Are you *serious*?"

He doesn't answer. He doesn't have to.

That horrible girl dumped my brother—my ultra-sensitive brother who loved her more than he'd loved any other girlfriend—on his birthday without explaining why. I clench my jaw and fists as tears sting my eyes. I hate her more than I did before. More than I've ever hated anyone.

"I'm sorry, B," I say.

"It isn't your fault, C. I just don't know what I did. It was something, obviously. Something big."

I shake my head. "No. She's stuck-up and she has a weird nose and she *sucks* and you can do so much better."

He tosses the last few centimeters of his joint out the window and smiles at me. It's a sad smile. A stoned smile. But at least he doesn't look completely miserable at this moment. "Her nose is kind of fucked up, isn't it?"

My head tingles a little, and I nod and smile back.

Maybe Mom was right. Maybe I am still the one person who can get through to him.

When we pull up in front of the town house, the minivan is in the driveway with every door open. I wheel my suitcase through the propped-open front door. Inside the small, tiled foyer, there's a flight of stairs leading up and another leading down.

"Look who's finally here!" Jacob yells as he barrels toward me from the upper staircase. "Losers!"

Bryan and I jump aside as Jacob runs past us. Tony traipses down after him. "Took you a while to get here," he says. "We made a stop for produce and still beat you by ten minutes."

"I picked the wrong line at the border," Bryan says. "As usual."

I keep my expression neutral. The truth is, our border crossing wasn't long at all, but he detoured into Whistler Village instead of coming straight here. I waited in the car and didn't ask questions when he came back twenty minutes later, but I'm positive that he scored his BC Bud. Otherwise, we'd probably still be there.

Tony nods in sympathy. "Been there, done that. Well, you two get to argue over the downstairs bedrooms. Go ahead and put your bags in your rooms and then come back up, all right? I can use help carrying things in, and your mom's trying to get the kitchen in order."

He didn't mention anything about Emma sleeping with me, like it isn't even on anyone's mind for this trip. Resentment toward Heather swells through me once again. If she were here, Emma and I would have no choice except to be in the same room because, technically, there wouldn't be enough beds.

Dragging my suitcase, I follow Bryan down to the bottom floor where there's a bathroom for us to share and two big rooms, each with a king-sized bed.

"Argue over bedrooms," Bryan mutters. "I think he's mixing us up with *his* bratty kids."

"Probably." I put on a smile and ball up my hands. "But I'm about to beat you down for the lavender bedspread."

He smiles back. "How about if I just let you have it? No fisticuffs required."

"Aww," I say, reaching up and patting the top of his head. "You're the best brother in the whole, wide world. And, of course, this has nothing to do with the fact that you like navy blue better, right?"

"Right." He pokes both of his cheeks to make dimples. "Or that Christmas is coming and my heart's grown three sizes today."

I push my suitcase into my room, and make my way up two flights of stairs to check out more of the town house. On the second floor, Mom is putting away groceries. She has bags and boxes of food strewn throughout the kitchen, dining area, and living room. I wander over to the sliding glass doors, and as I'm peeking out at the hot tub on the balcony, my sister comes running down the steps.

"Hey, Emma!" I call out. "I got us the lavender room on the bottom floor. Where's your luggage?"

"Oh!" She looks back and forth between me and Mom. "Aren't I supposed to sleep upstairs on the hide-a-bed by Jacob and Zach's room?"

Mom nods. "I think that will be best."

"Why?" I ask. "She can stay with me. We'll have a whole week of slumber parties. Do you want to, Em?"

"Yeah!" she says.

"Oh, I can see how this is going to go already," Mom says to me, shaking her head. "You know how difficult your sister is to sleep with."

Emma pouts. "But I'm not anymore. I've changed! I don't even snore now that my tonsils are out. I promise, I'll be quiet and lay flat like this all night long." She closes her eyes and stands at attention for a couple of seconds. "See?"

My sister is truly the noisiest, most restless blanket hog I've ever known. "It'll be fine," I say.

Mom shoves cereal boxes into a cupboard. "It actually would be nice if we could save that pullout bed on the third floor for Reece instead of having him down here. That way, the living room won't be all cluttered up with him and his things during our last two days. But it's totally up to you, Nicole."

I resist the urge to roll my eyes that she thinks Reece will "clutter up" the place. "Are you going to keep your promise and be still and quiet when I'm ready to sleep?" I ask Emma.

She nods, still grinning as her curls bob up and down by her face.

"Go get your stuff, then," I say.

"Yay!" Emma skips back upstairs.

"She *does* love hanging around with her big sis," Mom says. "I hope it all works out."

"It will. It's going to be great."

CHAPTER 7

It's our first day up on the mountain and soft, fluffy flakes are dancing around my face. This is the kind of snow that inspires people to smile and sing and feel all holiday-ish. No one else in my family seems to even notice it, though, because Tony had us rush to eat, rush to gear up, rush to get to the resort. Then, upon arriving, we got stuck waiting for tickets, waiting for the gondola, waiting for the chairlift. Tony's annoyed, Mom's annoyed, Bryan's annoyed. I'm annoyed that they're all annoyed.

"What did we expect, though?" Mom asks as we finally reach the front of the line for the Peak Chair. "It's two days before Christmas. I heard someone say that this is Whistler's busiest week of the year."

"We might want to wake up earlier tomorrow," Tony says. "Just in case it's worse."

Bryan elbows me. I don't have to look at him to know what

he's thinking because I'm thinking it too: The triplets are at snowboarding lessons for the next six hours, so Mom and Tony could be skiing anywhere on the mountain right now. Instead, they're tagging along with us. Why, why, why?

We all move forward together to get on the lift—Mom and Bryan on the outsides and Tony and me in the middle.

"And, we're off," Tony says, tucking his poles under his leg while Bryan and Mom pull down the safety bar. "Speaking of waiting. Bryan, did you happen to see if first semester grades are ready?"

Bryan's body tenses beside me. "They're up."

"And?"

"And . . . could be better, could be worse. I kind of screwed up my finals, but whatever."

Tony puts his elbow on the bar, and I flatten myself against the back of the seat as he talks over me. "We've discussed this so many times. You have to stay laser focused during under-grad if you want to get into a good law school. That's just the way it is."

"Who said I want to go to law school?" Bryan asks.

From Tony's other side, Mom's voice is loud and clear. "*You* did, Bryan."

Tony nods. "When we talked last summer, you agreed that it's a great career choice."

"Yeah, it's great for you. But there's no way I'm becoming an attorney."

"Where is this coming from?" Tony asks, frowning. "What's changed?"

I wince. I can't believe that after seeing how hard Bryan's taking the breakup with Heather, Tony asked that question and is forcing Bryan to have this conversation right now. It's as if he purposely waited to bring it up when there was no way to escape.

"Look," Bryan says. "Right now, I don't care. Okay?"

"It's not okay." Tony shakes his head. "It's a problem. You're letting *right now* ruin your chances—"

"Nothing is ruined." Bryan sits up straighter. "And, really, you have no clue. So do me a favor and save the tough-love speeches for your own kids."

Tony makes an irritated "Chhh!" sound. As he shifts to look at Mom, I take the opportunity to interrupt. "We're on vacation, you guys! Remember?" No one responds, so I go on. "There will be plenty of time to have conversations about grades and futures and everything else after we get home. Can't you let it go for seven days? Please?"

Tony looks at me and then at Bryan. "We'll talk about this later."

"*After* the trip, right?" I ask.

"Fine," Tony says.

"Do you agree, Mom?" I ask.

I can totally see Tony breaking his agreement by convincing her to do it instead. His job these days is to put together people's wills and stuff, so he hasn't been an actual courtroom attorney for years, but that doesn't mean he doesn't still strategize like one.

"Yes, Nicole," Mom says.

I jab the top of Bryan's leg. "And *you*. These snow conditions are a dream come true and you need to have some fun this week. I mean it."

"Fun. What's that?"

I flash him a big smile. "Only the best thing ever!"

He lifts one corner of his mouth and pokes my arm. "Whatever you say, Miss Bossy Sunshine."

A few minutes later, Bryan and I are sitting on the snow, clipping into our bindings alongside about a dozen other snowboarders.

"We'll meet you at the Big Red Express!" Mom calls to us as she and Tony ski away.

"Gotta love the quality bonding time," Bryan says.

"The family that rides the lift together, stays together," I say.

He smirks. "Where're we off to?"

"Somewhere that eventually brings us to them, I suppose. I'll follow you."

We push ourselves up from the ground and take off. Within seconds, he's way ahead of me. He glides through the powder and comes to a stop in front of a trail sign with two black diamonds on it. "Ready for the fun to start?" he asks, after I've caught up.

I scoot past him to glance down the hill, and my breath catches. From up here, the incline appears to be practically straight down. "If this is where fun is happening, then definitely not. I don't do double-black runs."

Bryan laughs. A real laugh. He honestly thinks I'm kidding. "I'll race you down, C. Winner gets . . . what? What's a good prize?"

I swallow. "Not going home in a body bag?"

"You're hilarious. Let's go."

If anyone else were asking—anyone in the world—I'd continue on the totally doable blue runs by myself and meet at the bottom. But it isn't anyone else. It's Bryan, who is actually trying to have a good time. Bryan, who needs my help keeping his mind off Heather.

I careen over the edge before he can register what's happening; the bigger head start I can get, the better. Within seconds, I know I've made a huge mistake. My brain screams: *slow down, slow down, slow down,* but the hill is so steep and icy that I can't even begin to catch an edge.

Bryan quickly overtakes me. I don't think he's hit the slopes since Thanksgiving of *last* year, but if he's feeling rusty, it's impossible to tell. "How does that saying about cheaters go?" he calls out.

"Bryan!"

I have no hope of winning the race—I never did—and I'm on the verge of hyperventilating as I zigzag out of control. I dodge a waist-high tree and scrape across a patch of exposed rock. I lean this way, that way, wobble, wobble, wobble . . .

Slam!

I'm sliding on my butt and then I crash onto my side. I'm screaming and rolling, rolling, rolling, rolling, rolling, rolling my way down the hill.

When the ground finally levels and my momentum halts, my heart is slamming in my chest. I pant, staring through my goggles at the sky.

Boots crunch over the snow. Bryan drops to his knees beside me and yanks off his goggles. "Shit! Coley, are you okay? Can you get up at all?"

I flex my arms, hands, legs, feet. "I'm not injured. If you

don't mind, though, I'm just going to lie here and die."

He lets out a loud breath. "Holy *crap*. That freaked me out. Are you sure you're all right?"

I prop myself up on my elbows. "I'm fine, see? Don't worry."

"Look where you came down," he asks, pointing up the hill. "I don't know how, but you managed to hit the only straight line without obstacles. You're going to be feeling those body slams tomorrow, but still, pretty lucky."

Actually, the body-slamming pain kicked in right away, but I don't want to say so and make him feel worse about it. "And who says 'cheaters never prosper'?" I ask, with a small smile. "We don't ever have to do that run again, do we?"

Bryan shakes his head roughly and takes my hands to pull me up. "No way."

"Okay, good."

The evening Fire and Ice show at Whistler Village that night is loud music, a loud emcee, and an even louder crowd. It's stunt snowboarders and skiers taking turns speeding down the hill and jumping through a huge, burning ring. It's fire dancers on both sides of the run swinging flaming torches, sticks, and whips. It's also a good enough mix of locals and out-of-towners so I don't feel like *too* much of a dorky tourist.

"All right!" the announcer yells in the mic. "These guys are working hard up there! Real hard, ladies and gentlemen. Whooooo! And give it up for a one-eighty! Yeah!"

Bryan ditched us right when we got here, and I'm standing up front on the snow-packed ground with the rest of my family. We're close enough to get powder sprayed through the safety blockade and the triplets are loving it. Even usually-mellow Zach has spent the past twenty or so minutes jumping around with Jacob and Emma while Mom, Tony, and I clap our gloved hands and cheer behind them.

"*You* could do that!" Emma yells over her shoulder to me, pointing at two dancers with flaming hoops spinning around and around and up and down their bodies. "You'd be even better at it than they are, I bet."

Mom nudges my arm, smiling. "She's right."

"Are you ready for this?" the announcer yells. "We're sending the entire crew through the ring of fire for you, Whistler! Rapid-fire time! One right after the other after the other after the other!"

For the grand finale, all the skiers and snowboarders perform their last backflips, front flips, and toe grabs while fireworks flash and boom and crackle over their heads. They line up together, facing us, as the emcee shouts all their names. We scream and clap some more.

Then his last words: "Thank you all for coming out, Whistler! See you on the slopes tomorrow!"

The crowd begins to break up. "Thank you all for coming *oot*!" Jacob says with a bow. "See you on the slopes to*moo*rrow!"

"Are we ready, then?" Tony asks, loudly.

I glance around. Bryan still hasn't come back.

Tony looks around too, and frowns. "Coley, where did your brother go?"

If I know Bryan, he's off sneaking a joint somewhere. "Bathroom?"

Tony glares at his watch. "I thought I'd made it clear that we're on a tight timeline."

"Story of our *lives*!" Jacob exclaims.

For once, Jacob and I are in agreement. It's annoying that Bryan left at the start of the show without a word to anyone, but the only reason it's a big deal is because Tony has over-scheduled us yet again.

Mom covers a yawn with the back of her hand. "Can't we do this sleigh ride another night?"

"No, Dawn," Tony says. "This is Christmastime, they're booked solid, and I prepaid."

"So, if we lived *here*," Emma says, "I think Coley should become a professional hula hooper of fire. And Daddy could become a ski instructor, and Mom could work at a gift shop or clothes store."

During all our trips, Emma plans new lives for us. In Hawaii, she decided that I should become a luau dancer. At Disney World, Rapunzel or Sleeping Beauty. In Las Vegas, a Cirque ballerina.

Jacob chimes in. "If we lived here, us kids would get to snowboard all day and never go to school again, right?"

"I'm not liking the sound of that," Mom says, tugging his knitted hat lower over his ears.

"Should someone call Bryan?" Tony asks.

"Or!" Emma says. "What if Daddy became a sleigh driver? Then we could brush and feed and ride the horses whenever we wanted."

Jacob spins around with his arms outstretched. A group of five guys—probably in their thirties—takes a few steps back.

"Those snowboarding guys were awesome," Zach says. "I mean, the skiers, too, but I like snowboarders better."

"Yeah," Jacob says. "They landed almost every jump. No big wipeouts like yours all day."

Zach sticks out his tongue. "Don't you mean, like you're going to have all *week*?"

"Please," Jacob says, with a wave of his hand. "I'm the jump freakin' master."

"Language," Mom says, with a sigh.

"What? I said *'freakin'* not *'fu—'*"

"Jacob, we get the picture," Tony interrupts. "Now, Coley. Your brother?"

My turn to sigh. "Fine, I'll call him."

I pull out my phone. The preview screen displays new texts that came in during the show:

Reece: I'm playing cards. Be jealous. Be very, very . . .

Noah: remind me 2 tell u a funny story when . . .

Ming: Xander got me earrings! My birthstone . . .

I can't read the full messages or respond since Tony's watching me, so I hit the button to dial my brother and hold the phone to my ear.

"Let me guess," Bryan says, without even a hello. "Tony's losing his shit. I'll be there in a second. Got you a consolation prize."

"For all my pain?"

He's already hung up, though. I spot him making his way across the snow toward us.

"We're so glad you could join us," Tony says.

Bryan presses a small white box into my hand. I'm too curious to wait so I kind of turn away from everyone, take off one glove, and lift the lid to peek. Inside are two stacks of Nanaimo bars with little squares of waxed paper between them.

I give a little squeal and grin at my brother. It's been a while since we've vacationed here, but he still hasn't forgotten that these chocolaty, custardy, Canadian treats are my favorite confections on the planet.

"What are you so excited about?" Emma asks. "What's in there?"

"Nanaimo bars!" I say.

"Yum!" Emma, Jacob, and Zach yell.

Tony scowls, probably because precious seconds are ticking away, but also, I suspect, because my brother got something just for me and gave it to me in front of the kids. And now I feel bad for bragging about it.

I look in the box again and count. Six. Bryan doesn't eat sugary stuff, so there's enough for the rest of us to each have one. "Dessert," I say, shaking the box. "Thank you for picking these up for everyone, B."

Mom gives him a sideways hug. "How very, very sweet. Pun intended, of course."

Bryan looks at me over her head and twists his lips into a those-really-weren't-for-them-but-that's-okay smile. "I have my rare moments, don't I?" he asks her.

"Yeah. *Very* rare," says Jacob.

Bryan laughs and the rest of us join in—even Tony.

"On that note," Mom says. "Doesn't the schedule say it's time for us to sing carols and get dragged around by horses in the snow?"

"It certainly does," Tony says, still smiling. "Shall we?"

CHAPTER 8

It is past eleven o'clock on Christmas night, and Emma is big-time breaking her promise to lie quiet and still.

"What *now*?" I ask as she throws back the covers on her side and climbs out of bed.

"Gotta pee!"

For the past five nights, she's fallen asleep almost as soon as her head's hit the pillow, but tonight she keeps getting up, saying that she's "thirsty," "hungry," or she "forgot something." And now she's using the bathroom excuse.

I wait until she's gone, then slide my phone out from under my pillow. The tiny, red light blinking in the darkness makes my heart jolt; a new text came since I checked two minutes ago.

> Reece: I need to NOT be awake right about now. Just wondering though: Have I ever told you that your beauty takes my breath away?

Those words on my tiny, bright screen. They take *my* breath away.

This all started as a game, but it feels more real every day. Reece and I haven't actually talked while I've been at Whistler, but the texts he's been sending have been getting bolder.

> Me: I have no guesses. I'm so bad at this! But thank you if you meant it. Have I ever told you that I've got my sights set on you and I'm ready to aim?

The toilet flushes and water runs in the sink. With my heart racing, I hit send and push my phone back under my pillow.

Will Reece take it seriously? Do I want him to?

Emma bangs her way back in and collapses onto the mattress. "I think Bryan's smoking or something. It smells weird by his door. Should we tell?"

"Bryan's old enough to do whatever he wants."

He's been acting less depressed for the past couple of days. I'm hoping that when he's used up his stash, he won't buy more.

"But smoking is bad for his health!" Emma says.

This is how different Emma is from me. Even when I was her age, the last thing I would ever do was go out of my way to get someone into trouble. "Being kept up all night by you is bad for *my* health. Why aren't you sleeping?"

"I just . . . can't."

"Because . . . ?"

"Ummmm," she says, dragging it out for about five seconds. "Because maybe they gave me Mountain Dew instead of Seven Up at the restaurant?"

I make a growling sound in my throat. The triplets are so not allowed to have caffeine. "You should have said something."

"But I never get to drink Mountain Dew."

"And there's a good reason for that. Remember when you and Jacob drank all that Dr Pepper and ended up running into each other and getting bloody noses?"

"That was a long time ago!"

"Not that long." My phone's on silent mode—not even vibrate—so I won't know when Reece texts back until I check the screen. "I'm going to sleep. So that means, don't talk to me anymore."

"Fine." She flips over so that her back is to me.

Pulling out my phone again, I tent the blankets over my head to hide the backlight while I check for messages. Nothing yet. I wait in text purgatory, keeping my head under the covers. Two minutes. Three minutes. Four.

Maybe Reece went to bed. I mean, he's leaving Kenburn to drive here in less than six hours so he does need to be asleep. But did he think my text was weird? I can't believe that I told him I was "ready to aim." It sounds way better in the song.

Five minutes. The red light flashes. Finally.

Reece: My song is by Ash, and yes, I meant it. I think you might have stumped me with your quote. :)

I smile at the little face.

Me: Yay! First time ever! It's "See You Again" by Miley Cyrus and I meant it too . . . only in a nice way instead of an assassin way. :)

Reece: Awesome! I wondered. Good night, Coley. See you soon.

Me: Good night Reece. <3

Feeling around on the wall for my charger, I accidentally knock a magazine off the nightstand, and it hits the floor. Emma's body jolts and she takes a loud inhale like I've startled her awake. Such a faker. "Now you're waking *me* up!" she says. "Who were you texting? Your boyfriend?"

I lean over the edge of the bed and plug in my phone. "That was Reece. A boy who's my friend."

"But he wants to be your boyfriend instead. And you want him to be, right?"

It's perfectly normal that a boy might drive to Canada to stay the night with a girl and her family simply because they're friends. I know it. But I'm sure that that is not what's happening here. I want something more with Reece. I'm almost positive that he does too.

I don't answer Emma's question. I close my eyes and take super-slow, loud breaths in and out through my nose to try to trick her into thinking I've drifted off.

She doesn't fall for it. "At dinner when Jacob called Zach a 'pussy fart' and Zach threw a piece of sweet-and-sour chicken at him and Mom made us all trade chairs, how come Bryan said, 'It's like living with chipmunks'?"

"He said '*The* Chipmunks,'" I say. "Like from the cartoon and those dumb movies."

"I don't get it."

"You know how on *Alvin and the Chipmunks*, everyone is always yelling Alvin's name like we're always yelling Jacob's? I think that's what he meant. Plus, Jacob's loud and gets all the attention just like Alvin, right?"

"But Bryan didn't say it was like living with Alvin. Does

that mean he thinks Zach and me are Chipmunks, too?"

"I don't know, Emma. I don't think he put a lot of thought into it. But Zach's sarcastic and brainy, so he's like Simon, right? And you're like Theodore, the cute, sweet one. So it fits."

"I guess so. But I don't want to be a Chipmunk with Jacob and Zach. I have to do karate and soccer because of them. And every year at school, I never get to be in my own class because they can't get along and there's only two teachers for every grade. I'm always stuck with one of them."

She switches back and forth between being Jacob's sidekick and nemesis so much that I never realized she feels this way. "Forget I said that then. You don't have to be Theodore."

She goes on as if I hadn't spoken. "People sometimes don't like *us* because of the way Jacob is. Bryan's our brother, even, and he thinks we're annoying."

"Bryan thinks the whole world is annoying."

"Not *you*. He likes you best 'cause you're his real sister instead of just a half."

She's right, but I don't want to agree and hurt her feelings. We lie in silence for several minutes. I can't tell if she's awake or not, so I whisper, "If you don't want to be a karate-mastering, soccer-playing Chipmunk, who do you want to be?"

"I don't know," she whispers back. "Maybe I want to swim."

"Like a mermaid in the ocean?"

She lets out a snort. "No. Like a girl on a swim team."

"Gotcha. Are any of your friends on the team? Maybe Mom could check to see if you can carpool with one of them."

"That's a good idea," she says, yawning loudly.

"I'm glad you think so. Are you falling asleep now?"

"I could."

"For reals, Em?"

"For reals."

And she's out. My turn now. If that's even possible.

CHAPTER 9

I'm nearing the end of the meditation portion of my yoga workout, which means I'm lying on my back with my eyes closed. Being calm and letting my thoughts "slip away" like the instructor on the television is telling me to do isn't easy. The only two TVs in this place happen to be in the fourth-floor master suite and in the living room, so I'm on my mat near where most of the rest of my family is eating breakfast a few feet away.

Yoga instructor: "Breathe. *Relax.* Experience the continuous flow of breath from your center . . ."

Jacob: ". . . checked in the mirror. I got a huge bruise on my butt."

Zach: "You were looking at your butt in the mirror?"

Emma: "Gross!"

Jacob: "Not as gross as the time you dreamed you were eating chocolate pudding . . ."

Yoga instructor: "*Close out* the rest of the world. Be at *one* with your inner self . . ."

Emma: ". . . never happened. You're so disgusting!"

Yoga instructor: "Take this time for *you* . . ."

Jacob: ". . . why you make such a big deal out of every little thing?"

Emma: "Because you bother me."

Yoga instructor: ". . . let your practice *absorb* into your being . . ."

Tony: "Come on, you two. Give it a rest."

Bryan: "Yeah, seriously."

I stand, press my hands together, bow my head toward the television, and say along with the instructor, "Namaste."

Feeling less calm and centered than I did when I woke up, I roll up my mat and lean it against the back of the couch.

Mom comes down the stairs in dark jeans and a cashmere sweater.

"A little overdressed for skiing, don't you think?" Tony says as he gets up from the table.

"I'm having my nails done today." Mom pours herself coffee and dumps hazelnut creamer into it. "I'm going shopping in the Village. Maybe I'll even see a movie. So no skiing for me."

We've had five actual days on the slopes and six activity-packed evenings. Everyone's a little bit tired, a little bit sore, and in Mom's case, at least, *a lot* over it.

Tony places his bowl in the dishwasher and shrugs as if Mom's announcement didn't totally stab his micromanaging heart. "I think that's a great plan, dear. Do what you have to do."

"Maybe the kids should take a day off too," Mom says. "You can go with them up to the tube park or something."

Over at the table, the triplets all look at one another with their eyes wide. "No!" Emma says. "We *have* to go to our lesson."

Zach nods. "It's *important*."

"The most important ever," Jacob says. "Max promised he's gonna teach us some tricks!"

It's amazing how they can scream at one another one minute, and then have one another's backs the next.

Mom puts her hands up in surrender. "All right, calm down. It was just an idea."

Tony turns to Bryan, who's on a barstool. "I guess you and your sister are stuck with me then. Should we do Blackcomb today?"

"Sure," Bryan says, looking my way. "Sound good?"

"It *does*," I say. "But the thing is, Reece is kind of a newbie, so I don't know if he can keep up with you guys. I think I should try a few runs with him and if it goes well, we can meet up. Okay?"

I brace myself while Mom frowns at Tony, but to my relief, neither of them argue. Bryan gives me a sidelong thanks-a-lot grimace and I mouth, "Sorry."

I am sorry to leave him with Tony, but my excitement over spending part of the day alone with Reece far outweighs it.

In front of the bathroom mirror, I put a fastener on the end of my braid and Bryan brushes his teeth. Reece has been on the road for hours so he should be here soon. Any minute. Any second.

"Cuh uh it ow?" Bryan asks.

"Huh?"

He points at his mouth.

Oh. *Can I spit now?*

I step aside so he can get closer to the sink.

Peering into my makeup bag, I debate what to use. I want to look put together, but also like I'm kicking back for vacation and not *trying* to look good. A little color on my cheeks is always nice, but if we go in the hot tub tonight, I'll probably regret eye makeup. So blush and lip gloss—

"Hey," Emma says, standing in the doorway. "Do either of you have extra energy bars? Jacob took the last one, and all that's left in the cupboard is that gross goo stuff that makes me want to gag."

Bryan unscrews the top of his miniature mouthwash. "I don't have any."

I'm about to give the same answer, but then I remember my Christmas present from Reece. "There's a box of granola bars in my backpack if you want one of those."

"Yay! Thanks!" She rushes away.

My thoughts swirl as I pat a little concealer underneath my eyes. What will it to be like when Reece gets here? Is it going to be weird to have him around my family? Will everyone be nice to him and manage to not do anything too embarrassing? Is he still going to like me? Is he going to kiss me—

"Wow," Bryan says. "You're like a million miles away."

I meet his gaze in the mirror. "Huh?"

"Exactly."

"Were you talking to me? What did you say?"

He gives my shoulder a squeeze. "Nothing important."

As he walks away, Emma comes back. "Why was this in with your granola bars?" she asks, handing me a small, black velvet case.

I stare at it. "I've never seen that before in my life."

Holding my breath, I pop the case open. Inside, hanging from a delicate silver chain, is an inch-long pendant—a giraffe pendant. I run my finger from its tiny pointy ears to its long neck to its textured spots. It's so cute and detailed and perfect. The perfect present for Reece to hide in a box of snacks.

And it hits me: The night that I gave him a stuffed giraffe, he gave me a giraffe necklace. It means something. It means *everything*.

"How do you think it got in there?" Emma asks.

I clasp the necklace behind my hair. "I'll give you a clue. Reece gave me those granola bars for Christmas."

"Ohh. And he put the real present inside. I told you he wanted to be your boyfriend."

"And you just know everything, don't you?" I say, grabbing my blush brush and dabbing the tip of her nose with it.

The doorbell rings.

Reece is here. He's here, he's here, he's here!

I haven't finished with my makeup, but I don't care. I toss the brush down and race for the stairs with Emma following.

Above in the foyer, Jacob says, "License and registration."

"Registration's out in the truck," Reece says. "I've got my license, though."

Jacob says, "Hand it over."

I reach the top of the staircase in time for Reece to pull his ID from his wallet and give it to my annoying little brother.

Sterling the Giraffe's head is poking out from the duffle bag hanging over Reece's shoulder. My heart gallops and I rush to stand beside Jacob.

"Hi!" I say to Reece.

"Hi!" he says.

I've been imagining this moment all week. I thought I was ready for it. Now I'm here and Reece is here. I'm looking up at him and he's smiling at me. I have zero doubt that everything is changing between us—that everything already has changed—and I don't how to act. I don't know where to stand, what to say, or *what in the world* I'm supposed to do with my arms.

"Jeez," Jacob says, reaching around Reece to push the door shut. "Are you going to stare at each other all day or what?"

My face gets hot and I resist the urge to shoot Jacob a dirty look. This isn't at all the reunion I was hoping for—especially the part where Emma and my nosiest family member are hovering. I touch my necklace and say to Reece, "I found this, like, two seconds ago. Thank you so much. I love it. Like, a lot."

He sags his shoulders, and his smile widens. "Oh, man. Finally. Every day this week, I've wanted to text you and say, 'Will you hurry up and open that box already?'"

Behind us, the second-nosiest person in my family clears his throat. "Tony DeLuca," he says, coming off the last step and shaking Reece's hand. "You must be Reece."

"He's Kinsey, Reece Oliver," Jacob says, waving the license in his hand.

Emma snatches it from him.

"I actually met you once before," Reece says to Tony. "At the Homecoming game?"

"Of course," Tony says.

"You didn't meet me," says Jacob.

"Or me," says Emma.

"True," Reece says, nodding.

My older brother ambles up the lower staircase. It's good timing so that Tony will have to back off. "Hey, Bryan," I say. "Come here really quick."

Instead, he goes into the laundry room, calling, "Anyone seen my gloves?"

"No!" Jacob yells back.

"Hey, Bryan!" I say again, but he doesn't even poke his head out.

"Kinsey, Reece Oliver, has green eyes," Emma reads. "And he's six-two and a hundred and fifty-six pounds."

She hands the license back to Reece, and he blushes as

he puts it away. "Actually," he says, "those numbers are a little outdated."

"Are they?" Tony glances toward me.

I think I can guess what he's thinking: If Reece has been driving long enough for his height and weight to have changed, maybe he's older than he looks. But, really, he's turning seventeen in February, so he's only eleven months older than me.

Tony motions up the stairs. "Reece, how about if I show you where you'll be sleeping and then you can get changed and ready to hit the slopes?"

"I'll show him," I say.

Tony shakes his head. "I've got this, Coley. Go see your mother for a minute, will you?"

The kids and Reece follow Tony upstairs right as Bryan comes out of the laundry room, carrying his snowboard jacket and pants.

"Reece is here," I tell him.

"So? Am I supposed to throw a parade?"

I stare at him, surprised by the fierceness in his eyes. "I wanted you to meet him. That's all."

His expression immediately softens. "I'm just messing with you." He drapes his arm around me. "Do me a favor, C?"

"What?" I ask, leaning sideways into him.

"Text me the second you guys can meet up. A day alone with Tony is like—"

"A day without unicorns and rainbows?"

He gives my braid a little tug. "I was going to say, a decade in hell. But, yeah, same thing for you, I guess."

CHAPTER 10

An hour and a half after Reece's arrival, we're riding a quad chair alone together. We *shouldn't* be alone when the lines are like this, but he got confused when it was time to load. At the last second, we were separated from the two skiers who were going to ride up with us.

I text Bryan to let him know that we're not going to be able to meet them at all today. I don't know how it will go over with him or Tony, but really, it's for their own good. Reece is rusty on a board. It seems like even green runs will be hard for him.

"The powder's been really good this week," I say as I zip my phone into a pocket and slide my gloves back on.

He nods, but keeps gripping the safety bar with both hands and looking straight ahead like he's been doing this whole ride so far.

"Are you okay?" I ask. "You've been kind of quiet since we left the house. Tony wasn't rude to you, was he?"

While they were upstairs, Mom gave a hushed speech for me only, during which she kept using the words "inappropriate" and "regret." As in, I need to make sure my behavior isn't the first of those or she'll make sure that I feel plenty of the second.

Reece shakes his head. "It was really nonthreatening as far as protective-dad lectures go. Believe me, I've heard worse."

I assume he's talking about Violet's father, but I can't bring myself to ask more. "Tony's actually my stepdad, not my dad."

"You mentioned that. He thinks of you like his daughter, though, right? Seems like it, at least."

It's never once occurred to me that Tony would think of me or Bryan as anything other than baggage that my mom brought into their marriage, but I don't want to tell Reece that. It's better for him to think things are totally normal and peaceful in our household.

Reece continues. "Anyway, we talked about music and stuff. He asked about jazz band. Told me what he has in his vinyl collection. That was mostly it. Noah had kind of warned me that your older clone—I mean, *mom*—is the tough one. Seems about right so far."

"My clone?"

"You must have noticed that you, your mom, and your sister have the same blond hair. Same brown eyes. The same face. So . . . clones. Sound about right to you?"

"No," I say, with a laugh. "For starters, my hair's straight and theirs is curly. But why were you and Noah talking about my mom, anyway?"

"You know, I don't remember. It all kind of started after the zoo, though. I knew that Noah took you to Homecoming, so when you and I first started hanging out, I tried to feel out whether he and the rest of the basketball team were going to kick my ass—"

"And he told you that it totally isn't like that with us?" I interrupt.

"Actually, he's never said one way or the other. But he's always turning around in pre-calc, trying to give me advice and everything. So I'm figuring that he must be cool with it."

This isn't the way Noah made it sound at all. "Advice about what? What does he say to you?"

"Hold that thought," Reece says with sudden panic in his voice. "What do I do?"

I follow his gaze straight in front of us. We're coming to the end of our ride. "Oh. Lift up."

He raises his leg up high in front and the board dangles below. He is *really* rusty.

"No," I say quickly. "Just a little. The tip only. Now scoot a little bit forward in the seat. When our boards touch the ground, stand up, put your free foot in the middle of the board, and let the chair push you forward, okay?"

"Okay, sure."

I wave downward so that the operator will slow the lift, but either he doesn't see or doesn't care, because we speed ahead. At the last second, as our boards make contact with the slick, hard-packed snow, I grab Reece's hand, thinking that I can help guide him. Instead, it seems to throw him completely off-kilter. His other arm thrashes around and he falls to the ground, taking me with him. We're a mess of limbs and bodies and snowboards.

"I'm sorry!" he says.

He crawls close to me, to accomplish what—I don't know. "Reece, we have to move!"

The lift stops right before the people behind are forced to ski over the top of us. Reece and I drag ourselves out of the way and flop down next to each other on a snow bank. A bunch of people are staring at us; a few are chuckling.

"Oh, wow," I say. "That is the first time I've ever had a lift stopped for me. And, you know, it really is as embarrassing as I always imagined."

Reece pushes his goggles up onto his helmet and lets out a loud breath. "I'm sorry about that."

"It's okay." I'm pretty sure I can feel bruises forming on top of the ones I already have. "Do you need help with your bindings?"

He nods slowly, like it takes all of his effort.

I unhook from my own board and kneel in front of him. "Hey, don't be all sad. I'm not upset or anything. Those guys in the booth should have been paying better attention."

"It wouldn't have mattered." Reece frowns down at his gloved hands. "Coley, I have to tell you something. I'm not really a snowboarder."

I mock-gasp. "So, you're a *skier*?"

"Not that either. The closest I've come is wakeboarding on the lake and playing snowboarding video games. Which . . . I figured out real quick isn't the same at all."

I push my own goggles up and look into his eyes. "So if you don't snowboard or ski, why did you want to do this today?"

"Well, because. I wanted to spend time with you. And I know. I *know* that that puts me on the wrong part of the creepy–cute scale and I'm sorry."

I can't help laughing at his miserable expression. "You don't have to be sorry. I want to spend time with you, too. I'm glad you're here. Really, really glad."

"Even though I suck and knocked you over?"

"We'll just call it even after the zoo."

"I like that plan." Reece glances at the people around us. "So what now?"

"There's pretty much two choices. We can sit here for the

rest of our lives or I can fasten your bindings and teach you how to get down this mountain."

"Option one it is then!" he says with a grin. "I mean, just kidding. I'm ready to do this. Kind of."

Reece and I are sitting on inner tubes, my arms are looped tightly around his legs, and we're screaming and laughing our way down a hill. "Told you tandem would be faster!" he yells from behind me.

It feels like we're going about fifty miles per hour, but obviously, we can't be anywhere near that. "Too! Fast!" I shriek into the wind.

We hit the bottom and gradually slow to a stop. Pushing ourselves to stand, we drag our tubes behind us, and head back to the line for the conveyor lift. "What was that?" Reece asks. "Our fourth time down already? See, I'm much better at this."

Our day at the mountain so far has included an exhausting three hours attempting to snowboard, a lunch break in the lodge, and now an hour at the tube park. I can tell that Reece is embarrassed about how things were going earlier, but for an absolute beginner on a board, he isn't as bad as he thinks. "You really were doing good by the end," I say. "If we had a couple of more days here, you'd definitely get it."

"I feel like I've spent all day on my butt."

"That's what snowboarding is like for everyone when they're learning, so that's perfect. Nobody likes a prodigy, you know."

"Yeah, you definitely couldn't mistake me for one of those."

My pocket dings for what's probably the fifteenth time today and I can't help groaning. Ming has been sending "Has he kissed you NOW?" texts, I swear, every half an hour and my blood pressure is rising. There were a few times while I was kneeling in front of him or helping him up that I'd thought he might kiss me, but he never did. Whenever Ming asks me about it, I keep wondering if it's ever going to happen, if I should be doing something different in order to *make* it happen.

"Who do you think this one's from?" I ask Reece. "Ming? Or, perhaps, my dear friend, Ming?"

He laughs, but I have a feeling that he wouldn't find it so funny if he had any clue what she's been bugging me about.

I pull out my phone, bracing myself. "And the winner is! Oh . . . actually, it's Piper."

Piper: Hi, we need to set up a game plan for you and Alejandra. Call me?

This is worse than Ming's questioning. I scrunch up my nose and tilt the screen for Reece to read. "If I tell Piper that I never got this message, will you back me up?"

"Sure," he says, shrugging.

"Or, how about this?" I type quickly and send Piper a response.

> Me: Hi! Good to hear from you! I'm in line to ride an inner tube down a hill. Coming home from vay-cay in 2 days & will call you then :)

Within seconds, my phone rings. It's Piper.

"Okay, so that didn't work," I say.

"Sorry to bother you," Piper says when I answer.

"It's okay. Just talk fast, will you?"

"How are you doing? Are you having a good trip?"

"Pretty good—"

"And how's Bryan? I heard about his girlfriend. Is he doing okay?"

I resist the urge to hang up. Sometimes her obsession with him is so irritating. "He's still the same old Bryan," I say without emotion.

"That's good. You should make sure he's coming over for New Year's. I mean, it's tradition, and he skipped last year, so—"

"Piper, I hate to cut you off," I say in a rush, "but it's almost my turn."

Grinning, Reece sweeps his arm toward the dozens of people who are waiting ahead of us. I smile back, but wince inwardly at having told such a stupid lie right in front of him.

"Sorry!" Piper says. "Okay, so really quickly then. Your meeting with Alejandra. I'm thinking a neutral, public place. That coffee shop at the bookstore? Or how about Starbucks? Should we aim for the twenty-eighth? Maybe around two? I'll set it up with Alejandra if that works for you, and then we'll all meet there."

"Did Alejandra actually tell you that she wants to do this?"

"I don't care what she wants," Piper says. "I don't care what you want either. I've worked too hard to just sit back and watch my squad fall apart my senior year. So I'll text you with the details when she confirms. I'll be the mediator. You're both going to show up and make nice, and then we'll all be happy."

"Okay, then," I say, trying to keep the skepticism out of my voice. "I have to go now. Bye."

"Don't forget to talk to your brother!"

I end the call and let my head fall back as I stare at the gray sky.

"What's up?" Reece asks.

"Just Piper being Piper. Basically, she wants to force Alejandra and me to make up."

"What happened there, anyway? I used to see you two together all the time. But not for the past few months, right?"

"Since right around when you and I started hanging out, actually." I bump my hip into the side of his thigh. "So it's probably your fault."

"Oh, okay. Like how you lost your accent because of Xander?"

"Exactly like that!"

I'm ready to move on to another subject, but Reece is watching me with curiosity, so I wave my hand and say, "It's stupid. Alejandra broke up with her boyfriend in October and was acting all crazy and weird afterward. We kind of had a fight, and it keeps dragging on."

"What was the fight about?"

I pretend to think about it for a few seconds. "You know, I don't even remember."

I'm lying again, of course. I definitely haven't forgotten that Saturday morning when Alejandra showed up at practice and sobbed all over the locker room. It was right after she and Derrick had been together for three months, and not only had she lost her virginity to him the night before, she'd also dumped him.

From what I could understand, she was nervous, but decided that she'd be okay doing everything except *it*, so she let him go down on her. In the middle of that, she stopped him and said that they should have sex instead. Afterward, she told him she never wanted to see him again.

I couldn't figure out why she'd done any of that. It made no sense. While I tried to ask her questions, she started screaming that the whole thing was my fault. *How could you let Pedro do that to you? Why did you say that it felt good? It's totally disgusting and embarrassing!*

And that was exactly the moment that I was done being friends with her.

"Maybe Piper will get her way," I say, putting on a smile for Reece. "Or maybe Alejandra and I will be mad at each other forever. Stayed tuned for the oh-so-dramatic conclusion."

"Don't stress over it." He touches my shoulder. "You'll fix things. My mom once got into an argument with her sister over who was buying the bike rack for a trip. They wouldn't talk to each other for three months. My dad was like, 'You're pissed off because of a *rack*?' They finally started speaking again and everything's been cool ever since. So, see?"

"See, what? Alejandra and I aren't the only ridiculous females in the world?"

He grins. "You said it, not me."

My phone rings in my pocket. I put my finger to my temple and motion like I'm pulling the trigger. "I'm so sorry about this."

"No worries," Reece says. "This is what I get for hanging out with such a popular girl, I guess."

"I'm taking this call and then it's going on silent mode for the rest of the day. Promise."

I check the screen. This time, it's Tony. "Coley," he says in a strained voice. "There's been an accident. Someone crashed into Emma and her leg might be broken."

"*What?* Broken?"

Reece is watching me with his eyes open wide, and I frantically mouth, "Emma," while pointing at my leg.

"We don't know for sure yet," Tony says in my ear. "But I was able to get ahold of your mom and she's with your sister in the ambulance now. I'm going to head to the hospital too. I'm hoping you and Reece can take the boys back to the town house and keep an eye on them until we get home?"

"Of course."

"It'll probably be at least a couple of hours. Bryan rode with us today instead of taking his own car, so he's stranded in the Village. I cannot for the life of me get him to pick up his phone, but I left him a message to call you when he's ready for a ride."

I nod, even though Tony can't see me.

"I appreciate your help with this," he says. "Zach and Jacob are waiting outside the ski rental building. I gave Zach a key card so you'll be able to get into the town house, and I'll let you know when we have news."

"We need to go?" Reece asks as I end the call.

"I'm sorry. But, yes. My brothers are in need of the Reece Kinsey taxi service."

"No problem." He takes my pull rope in the same hand as his and leads me out of line.

CHAPTER 11

At the town house two hours later, Jacob, Zach, Reece, and I are up to our chests in hot, steaming water and have icicles forming in our hair.

Reece is shirtless beside me, and I can't help sneaking glances. He isn't super built, but from what I can see in the light spilling out of the dining room, his shoulders, pecs, and arms are definitely toned.

"I'm hungry," says Jacob.

"Me too," says Zach.

"I have an idea," I tell them. "Why don't you both go inside and make something for everyone? Let us know when it's ready."

"Nice try, Coley," Jacob says, looking back and forth between Reece and me with narrowed eyes.

This has all been going on for at least thirty minutes, and my brothers' refusal to leave us alone makes me want to scream. Truly, this is not how I want to spend this precious time without parents. Reece and me in a hot tub? Yes! With my little brothers? No, thank you very much.

In frustration, I slap at the water in front of me, and it hits Jacob's face.

"Hey!" He splashes back and soon we're all churning water up and ducking our heads.

"Hang on!" Zach calls out over the splashing water. "Coley's phone's ringing."

We all stop as quickly as we started and I lean way over the edge of the hot tub. With my hand still wet, I grab my phone from one of the deck chairs and listen to my very annoyed-sounding mother as she gives me the scoop on the other end.

"Well?" Jacob asks when I set my phone down less than a minute later.

"Well," I say, settling in again, much closer to Reece this time. "It was a clean break, Emma's in pain, but doing okay, Mom's mad, and they ordered Chinese takeout for dinner. They'll probably be here in fifteen minutes."

"Chinese two days in a row?" Jacob says. "Why not pizza?"

"I don't know. Why don't you go call and ask her?"

Once again, he makes no move to get out.

"Who's Mom mad at?" Zach asks.

I shrug. "She just had that tone of voice, you know?"

Jacob and Zach both nod. They've heard it a million times too.

Something hits my hand under the water. I start to pull back, but then I realize that it's Reece's hand wrapping around mine, and I relax.

"What's a 'clean break'?" Jacob asks. "Is that good?"

"I don't think breaking your leg is ever a good thing," Zach says.

"Actually, it's really bad," Reece says. "They call it a 'clean break' when your limb gets broken *clean off*. Get it?"

Jacob and Zach look at each other for a moment before Jacob says, "Nuh-uh."

Still underwater, Reece's fingers trace the length of mine. His fingernails run down my palm to my wrist, and my heart goes absolutely crazy.

"Yeah-huh," Reece says. "You know those pirates with wooden peg legs? Clean breaks, all of them. That's what Emma's coming home with too. Which sucks, but you know, it isn't the end of the world."

Jacob lowers his eyebrows as he seems to continue to ponder.

A slow grin spreads over Zach's face. "You are *so* lying."

Reece grins back. "You can go inside and look it up online if you don't believe me."

I remain perfectly still—unable to speak, to breathe. Reece's fingers are all over mine underwater, slowly massaging and pressing and intertwining. No one has ever held hands with me this way.

"What does it really mean, Coley?" Zach asks.

"I'm not a doctor." I'm amazed that I can sound so normal right now. "Maybe that the bone isn't splintered and will heal easier?"

Jacob slides his head all the way underwater and then bobs back up. "There's so many bubbles in here. I bet if someone farted, we wouldn't be able to tell."

"Don't you *dare*," I say, raising a finger on my free hand.

Zach and Reece laugh.

"We had a Jacuzzi outside on the deck when I lived in Alaska," Reece says. "Whenever my cousin would visit in the winter, we'd have all these competitions—"

"Farting competitions?" Jacob asks.

Reece laughs again. "No. We'd see who could hold their breath underwater longer. Or we'd run out in the snow while we were soaking wet." Reece's thumb slow dances with mine. "I think we should have a hot-tub-to-snow-angel competition right now."

"What's that?" Jacob asks.

"It's when you and Zach get out of the water, run

downstairs, lie on the snow, and see who can thrash your arms and legs around for the longest."

"That's sounds *cold*." Zach lifts his hands up into the steam as if to check the temperature.

"That's the point of it," Reece says. "Shock your body. See who's the toughest. If you guys run around to the back, your sister and I will be the judges from up here."

"No way," Jacob says. "I'm only doing this if we *all* do it."

Reece looks at me. "Do you want to?"

"Of course," I say. "Frostbite sounds lovely."

He smiles. "The bravest girl I know."

"Sweet! Let's go," says Jacob.

He climbs out of the hot tub and Zach follows. As they head inside with water running down their legs, Reece says quietly to me, "I can tell you right now that you won't be in the snow long enough for frostbite. We'll be lucky if we can last ten seconds."

"That's reassuring," I say.

I don't want to let go of Reece's hand, I don't want to get out of the water, and I especially don't want to make an angel in the snow, but I hoist myself out anyway, slip on my flip-flops, and wrap my towel carefully around my body. I have on my red bikini instead of my sporty, blue one-piece. As soon as we're finished with this little contest, I'm going to have to hurry and get dressed so that Mom and Tony won't catch me in what they'll probably think of as an "inappropriate" swimsuit to wear around Reece.

As he steps out behind me, my phone rings. This time it's my older brother.

"Thanks for calling," Bryan says as I answer.

I head into the dining room to get out of the cold. Jacob and Zach have already run downstairs, but Reece kind of hovers at the top with his towel around his waist as if he wants to wait for me, but isn't sure if I want him to. "Was I *supposed* to call?" I ask Bryan.

"Would've been nice if you'd let me know what's going on."

My stomach drops. It's dark outside and the ski lifts closed back while Reece and I were still at the tube park. Which means that my brother has been waiting around with his gear for who knows how long. Why didn't he call me sooner?

"Bryan, I'm sorry. I thought Tony said that he left you a message."

There's silence for a moment, and then Bryan says, "He did."

"Oh." I don't know why, but I can't keep up with this conversation. "So did you know that Mom and Tony were with Emma at the hospital, and we're watching Jacob and Zach until they get back?"

"I thought someone was supposed to pick me up."

"Reece can come get you." I glance at Reece, who nods. "Or, actually, Mom let me know that they're grabbing Chinese food and then coming home. If you call them now, they can probably swing by on the way."

Bryan sighs in my ear. "Are you kidding me? Chinese *again*? How about . . . do you want to have dinner with me at that sports bar at the base of the slopes?"

"With Reece, too?"

"Obviously."

I hold the phone away from my mouth. "Reece, is it okay with you if we eat with Bryan in the Village?"

"Sure," he says.

"Okay," I say to Bryan. "But we can't leave the boys until everyone gets back. And I need to wash the chlorine out of my hair. We can be there in maybe forty minutes."

"I'll get a table. Just hurry, okay? Don't be all picky about your makeup and everything."

"Okay, *Mister* Bossy."

We hang up, and as I'm setting my phone on the table, Jacob yells from downstairs, "What're you guys waiting for? Come on!"

Reece and I make our way to the bottom of the stairs, and Zach pulls the door open and jumps back. A gust of wind makes the goose bumps all over my body stick up even more.

"We're really doing this?" I ask, pulling my towel tighter.

"It'll be quick," Reece says. "And mostly painless."

I follow him out and glance at the boys. Zach steps back into the foyer, out of sight. Jacob looks right at me and shouts, "Suckers!"

The door slams shut with the two of them inside and the two of us outside.

"Hey!" I yell. "What are you doing?"

I try to twist the door handle, but it's locked. "Jacob DeLuca! Open the door! Right. This. Second."

He laughs on the other side.

"Did he really lock us out?" Reece asks.

"Yup." I hit the door. "Open up! Now!"

"Have fun out there, you lovebirds!" Jacob shouts.

"Come on, you guys!" Reece calls out. "This is not cool."

We're greeted with silence.

Under the porch light, I pound on the door until my fists hurt. Reece rings the doorbell every few seconds and hops up and down on the stoop in his bare feet. Less than two minutes out here already feels like hours.

"Your brothers are supervillains," Reece says.

My towel is sliding, so I pull it tighter around my chest and retuck one end at the middle. "I'm going to murder them both."

"Literally?" he asks.

"Literally. Knives and carnage are up next on the agenda. Just as soon as, you know, we figure how to get back in."

"There's that tiny detail." He steps close to me and runs his hands briskly up and down my arms. His hands aren't especially warm, so it doesn't help, but his touch jumpstarts my heart.

"You're wishing you were home right about now, aren't you?" I ask.

It's a silly and desperate question, but I need to hear him say that he wants to be here, that he wants to be with *me*.

"I'm going to have to have my feet amputated if this goes on too much longer, but it isn't so bad that I wish I were at home," he says.

That wasn't quite what I was hoping for. "You getting frostbite is not an option." I gesture down the street. "I'm wearing shoes, so I'm going to run to the main office and see if I can get them to unlock the door for us."

"You don't have to do that," he says. "I'm sure that Jacob will let us back in any second."

"*I'm* sure that you don't know him very well."

Reece drops his towel on the ground, stands on it, and then folds it over his feet. "There. See? I'm out of the snow so you don't have to leave."

"Meanwhile, the rest of you is going to freeze."

"Or . . . not." He takes my hands, draws me toward him, and wraps his arms around me. I loosen my towel and hold both ends behind his back so that we're sharing it. My heart thumps against his ribs and his thumps into my collarbone.

"This might be shaping up to be our best day ever now," he says as we shiver against each other.

That's what I wanted to hear. I look up at him. "Really? This is better than giraffes and ice cream?"

"You don't think so?"

With his face this close to mine, he's just eyes, a nose and cheeks that are pink from the cold, and upturned lips. I smile back so big, it almost hurts. "I'm going to have to think about that."

"Sure. Let me know when you decide."

He slides a section of damp hair off my face, and I float up to my tiptoes so that our noses are nearly touching. Seconds, months, decades pass until finally—*finally*—Reece bridges the centimeters between us. My eyes fall shut and our lips brush together: once, twice, three times. As we deepen the kiss, his mouth is hot against mine. He tastes spicy, like cinnamon. Our tongues touch. Unlike what I've told my friends, I've never done this. I hope I'm getting it right, that he feels as warm and tingly inside as I do.

We break away and I'm breathless. Reece watches me, expectantly.

"You're right," I say, resting my cheek on his chest. "Totally our best day ever."

Seconds later, our moment on the stoop is interrupted by tire chains grinding over the snow and headlights beaming at the town house. I squint as Mom's minivan comes to a stop next to Bryan's car. Reece and I let go of each other and I fix my towel again. "We're rescued," I say.

I'm too hyped up to stress about the lecture I'm going to get from Mom. Her eyebrows practically lift off her forehead as she climbs out and hands Tony her keycard, but it's Tony who says, "What in the *world* are you two doing out here?"

"Well," I say, "We were going to have a snow-angel-making contest with Jacob and Zach, but they decided to lock us out instead."

"Oh, jeez." Tony shakes his head. I can't tell if he thinks I should have predicted that they would do something like this, but I don't *think* that's what he's thinking. "How long have you been out here?"

"Not long," Reece says. "About five minutes."

"It felt like longer," I say. "We came from the hot tub to *this*."

Tony lifts Emma from the backseat, and she holds on to his neck while her legs hang over his arms. He leans back inside for a moment and pulls out a set of crutches.

"Do you need me to help with anything?" Reece asks.

Tony gestures toward Mom opening the hatch, so Reece rushes across the snow on his poor, frozen feet. Tony makes his way up to me carrying Emma, and I take the crutches from him while he swipes the keycard. When I step inside behind him, it's already much warmer than outside, but not enough to keep me from continuing to shiver.

I follow Tony upstairs. After he sets Emma on the couch, I help adjust pillows behind her back and under her leg.

"How are you feeling?" I ask her.

Her eyelids look heavy. "Tired. Really . . . tired."

Tony rubs the top of her head. "They have her on pain killers. She'll probably be asleep again any minute."

I've never broken anything, so I don't know whether Emma needs to keep her leg propped up all night or what. I seem to remember that that's what Bryan had to do when he broke his ankle a couple of years ago. "I can sleep up here in the living room tonight if she needs the bed to herself," I say.

"We'll figure something out," Tony says.

Reece and Mom walk past and set the bags of Chinese food on the counter.

"Where's Bryan?" Mom asks.

I explain about him asking Reece and me to meet him in the Village for dinner. Mom purses her lips as she pulls a stack of plates from the cupboard.

"Your mom told you that we were bringing food for everyone," Tony says.

"I know," I say. "But Bryan wanted something different. And he still needs a ride no matter what."

Reece says, "Um, if it's all right, I'd like to go take the hottest shower of my life now."

Tony chuckles. "You know where it is."

As Reece runs upstairs, Jacob comes barreling down—fully dressed again—with Zach behind him.

"Oh!" Jacob yelps, jumping aside.

"'Oh!' is right," Mom snaps. "Get down here!" She waits with her hands on her hips. When both of my little brothers are standing in front of her, she continues. "It is not *ever* okay to lock your sister outside. Especially when she's wearing a wet bathing suit in the middle of winter, for God's sake. What were you *thinking*?"

"We didn't know the door was locked!" Jacob blurts out.

By his expression, I can tell that it was the first excuse that came to his mind and he already knows that it isn't going to work.

I roll my eyes. "And us ringing the doorbell, like, two hundred times didn't give you the hint?"

Zach stares silently at the floor, but Jacob never gives up, even when he knows he doesn't stand a chance. "It was a joke," he says to Mom. "And I was coming down to let them back in."

"It wasn't funny," I say. "And, obviously, you were too late."

Mom narrows her eyes. "Nicole, you need to go put some clothes on. Your lips are turning blue right in front of me. And Jacob, sit *down*. You too, Zach. When you're finished eating, you can both go to your room for the rest of the night."

"Mom!" they say in unison.

"Don't 'Mom' me. I'm not in the mood for it right now."

On that note, I run downstairs for my own hot shower.

CHAPTER 12

The lighting inside the restaurant is dark, but instead of feeling moody, the atmosphere is upbeat with a lot of loud talking and laughing going on. The greeter leads us through the crowded dining area to a booth where Bryan is slumped over a half-eaten burger, some scattered fries, an empty pitcher, and an almost-empty glass of beer. "There you are," he says, barely glancing up.

"You've already eaten?" I ask.

"Sorry. Got tired of waiting."

He doesn't sound sorry; he sounds, well, *drunk*.

"We can leave if you're ready," I say. "There's actually lots of food at the house."

"Who said I was ready?" Bryan sweeps his hand out in front of him. "Have a seat. Stay awhile."

The greeter lifts the menus she's holding. "So you need these or . . . ?"

I look at Reece. He shrugs and nods at the same time like he's fine either way, so I sit and he slides in beside me. The woman takes our drink orders: I request water with lemon, Reece asks for a Coke, and Bryan taps the side of the pitcher and says, "I could use another of these."

"Of course," she says, swiping it from the table and hurrying away.

It's weird to me that Bryan can legally order alcohol in Canada. It's weirder that he managed to down an entire pitcher before we got here. I don't know how many glasses that would amount to, but I'm guessing at least five.

We sit in silence for a few moments while Reece and I look over the menu.

"So what's up with Emma?" Bryan asks, slouching back. "Did she get the air-cast-and-crutches treatment?"

I nod. "She was conked out on the couch when we left."

"Sucks," Bryan says. "She's going to hate it. I spent half of my senior year on crutches. Got so sick of those things."

A server comes over to drop off our drinks and try to convince us to get an appetizer. After he walks away, I say to Bryan, "Sorry about today. How was it hanging out with Tony?"

"We split up after a couple of hours because he couldn't keep my pace." Bryan pours himself another glass of beer.

"What about you guys?" He looks back and forth between us. "Seemed from your text like you were having big problems."

"Just at first," I say quickly, wishing he hadn't mentioned that; I don't want Reece to be embarrassed. "It got better."

"A *little* better," Reece says, correcting me with a smile. "I was definitely holding her back, though."

Bryan takes a long swallow. "How is it that we never ran into you all day? Were you even on Blackcomb?"

"Yes," I say. "But we were taking it easy on Crystal Road and Green Line. We also went to the tube park, which was really fun, but then Tony called and said I had babysitter duty, so that was the end of that."

"I can't believe you wasted your last day on bunny hills and inner tubes," Bryan says, frowning. "You could have gone on some insane trails with me."

As if I was supposed to just leave Reece alone and go off with Bryan? That isn't what he would have done to Heather if she were here; it isn't what *anyone* would do. "I already went on all the trails that I wanted to. I don't need nonstop excitement, you know."

"Clearly," Bryan says, looking straight at Reece.

I don't know what to say when he gets like this. He's looking for an argument and I'm not going to give it to him.

While I'm trying to think of something else to talk about,

Reece asks Bryan, "So how did your ankle heal up, anyway? Are you playing basketball in college?"

Confusion flickers across Bryan's face, and I realize for the first time that Reece must know Bryan, since I've never told him about Bryan being on the team.

"I played on JV for one year. Which was when you were a senior," Reece says, answering the unasked question. "We practiced in the same gym. Well, until you got hurt."

"Holy shit." Bryan sets his half-empty glass down hard and leans in to study Reece. "I thought you looked kind of familiar. You were that freshman who was going out with D.T. Johnson, right?"

"Her name is *Violet* Johnson," Reece says. "But yeah, that was me."

"What's 'D.T.' mean?" I ask.

"Deep Throat," Bryan says with a snicker.

"Oh," I say.

I shouldn't have asked. I really didn't need to know. More importantly, I can tell by the way Reece is staring at his hands folded on the black tablecloth and clenching his jaw that this is a bad subject for him, too.

I glare at Bryan, but he doesn't seem to notice or care. "That chick," he says. "Whoa. She hooked up with, like, five of my friends. Not all at the same, though. I don't think so, anyway." He leans back again. "God, I haven't thought about Violet in forever. How's she doing these days? Or should I say, *who's* she doing?"

"She's fine," Reece says, looking him in the eye. "She graduated last year and she's going to school in California."

"Next time you see her, tell her 'hi' from me." Bryan sets his napkin by his plate and stands. "I'm going to take a piss now."

I watch him amble away and then turn to Reece. "I'm so sorry."

He shrugs. "You don't have anything to apologize for."

I wave my hand in the direction Bryan headed. "I'm the one who brought you here and my brother happens to be in a really bad mood. So there's that."

"It isn't your fault. Guys have been giving me crap about Violet since I was fourteen, so I'm kind of used to it."

"That's a long time," I say lightly.

"It definitely is. Not even half as long as she had to deal with it, though."

My brother dredged all this up and then walked away. I wish I could too, but I can tell by Reece's face that he wants to discuss it further.

How do I do this, when all I want is to forget that Violet was important to Reece long before I was?

"Have you . . . heard from her lately?" I ask.

"Not really," he says, shaking his head. "We've sent a few e-mails, but it's been a while."

I nod and draw squiggly lines in the condensation on my water glass using my fingertip.

"Is this too weird?" Reece asks. "Talking about my ex-girlfriend?"

"No," I lie. "It's fine."

"Okay, good. Things are different for her now, but when she was at our school, she put up with a lot of people saying a lot of things for a long time. She had this attitude like she didn't care. I know she did, though."

Maybe I can do this. "You two broke up when she left for college?"

"No. It was in May. Before she graduated. By then, she'd been pretty much been done for six months already."

I stop decorating my glass and look at Reece. "Done with *you*?"

"With me. With everything having to do with Kenburn. She wanted out, you know? And she deserved to get out. I never blamed her for that."

He's so calm, unlike Bryan over his breakup. Of course, Reece has also had all of these months to process it.

"It was hard, though, wasn't it?" I ask. "For you?"

"At first. I'd been with her, literally, since a few weeks after I moved here. The very start of my freshman year. I was a scrawny dork with braces, who never could figure out what she saw in me." He smiles. "Now, of course, the braces are off so I'm just a scrawny dork."

"That's not true." Smiling back, I poke his bicep through his shirt. "You've got guns under those sleeves."

"BB guns, maybe. And I notice that you didn't say I'm *not* a dork."

"Oh, didn't I?" I pinch my fingers together and motion like I'm zipping my lips closed.

Reece laughs. "Anyway. It all worked out and I'm glad for her. She doesn't have any jackasses in her life calling her 'D.T.', so that's good stuff."

The way he's talking, I can see that Ming was right about Reece being over Violet. The best part, though—the part that makes me like him even more—is that he doesn't seem fazed by whatever happened before that got her the nickname "D.T." He wasn't upset with *her*, only with how other people treated her.

"About the jackasses," I say. "What Bryan said to you just now. I want you to know that he isn't usually like that."

Reece lifts his eyebrows.

"He really isn't," I insist. "His girlfriend broke up with him a couple of weeks ago on his birthday and he's not dealing very well. As you can see."

There's a long pause before Reece says, "That's rough, but . . ."

He shrugs and looks away without finishing his sentence. I can tell he's thinking that I'm making excuses and Bryan's a jerk. It stings, but I understand why he'd feel that way. I don't get the impression that Reece lashed out at everyone after things ended with him and Violet. With Bryan, it's as if it doesn't even occur to him to *not* take it out on the whole world.

"I know that he comes across badly sometimes," I say. "The truth is, he's really sensitive and gets super depressed."

"Oh." Reece nods. "Yeah. My mom has that. She swears by vitamin D."

"No, it isn't a vitamin thing." I pause, wondering whether I should say more. If Reece can share personal things with me, I can tell him this. I *will* tell him. "It's because of our real dad."

"What do you mean?" Reece asks, frowning in confusion.

Now what have I started? I take a deep breath and speak in a rush. "I don't remember him, actually. I just know that our mom pretty much fled New Zealand with Bryan and me. Bryan remembers what happened and has bad memories and everything."

"I'm sorry. I had no idea."

Reece doesn't look weirded out, but I kind of wish I could take my words back anyway. This is too much.

Before he can ask further questions, our server comes back to take our orders. I've never appreciated an interruption as much as I do this one. I ask all about salad dressings, soups of the day, and Italian soda flavors. I even change my order twice so that I can put as much time between our last conversation and our next one.

As soon as the server leaves, Reece turns back to me, looking like he wants to pick up where we left off.

"You know what?" I say. "I should"—I point past him—"be right back."

"Sure." He scoots aside so that I can step out of the booth, and I hurry through the dining room to find the bathroom.

Stupid, stupid, stupid.

I shouldn't have told Reece that stuff. I want him to see my family as normal—not scandalous and dramatic—but because of Bryan, I'm failing big-time.

Standing in front of the mirror, I admire my necklace and try to think of a new topic for when I get back to the table. Maybe I won't need one, though. Maybe Bryan will be there and in a less jerky mood. Maybe conversation will flow without awkwardness. Maybe the worst of the night has already happened.

I can only hope.

Behind me, the door flings open and two college-aged girls stumble in, doubled over with laughter. They're both wearing little skirts and big jewelry, and are really pretty.

"There's a sign on my forehead, isn't there?" the blonde asks. "There *has* to be."

The brunette clomps over to the sink beside me in her high-heeled boots. "I swear there isn't. Check it."

The blonde stands next to her and leans in close to the mirror, touching her forehead like she's truly trying to find something. "You're right. Is it my aura then? How does this keep happening to me? I mean, I might be an American—"

"There's no 'might' about it," the brunette says.

"Okay, but my *God*! That doesn't mean that I'm giving it up to every foreign guy who wants me. It takes more than a cute smile, a nice body, and a hot accent to get into these pants." The blonde gives her own butt a pat.

"What does it take, then?" her friend asks in a teasing voice.

"How about a cute smile, nice body, hot accent, and *not* being a creepy creep," the blonde says. "Because, bitch, I have standards."

They dissolve into giggles again. I can't help kind of laughing with them for a second, but then I'm hit with an unexpected pang of loneliness. This used to be Alejandra and me. I mean, we aren't flashy like these girls, and would never have called each other "bitch"—not even as a joke—but all the silliness and teasing and hiding in the bathroom to talk about weird guys? So us.

The brunette dabs tears of laughter from the corners of her eyes and then turns to me as if she's noticing me for the first time. "That is *such* a cute purse. Where'd you get it?"

I look down at the pink and black Kate Spade on my arm. "Thanks. It was a Christmas present from my brother."

"Wow," she says. "Where can I sign up for a brother like that?"

"Seriously." The blonde puckers up to smooth on red lipstick. "Mine is useless. He sits in my parents' basement all day, getting high and playing video games."

"Oh, no." I flash a sympathetic smile toward her in the mirror, and fall silent. I don't know why it even matters—I'll never see them again—but I like that these girls believe that Bryan is the awesome, purse-buying type of brother and not the pot-smoking-in-the-basement sort.

"So, are we doing this?" the brunette asks her friend, motioning toward the door.

"There aren't any windows to climb out, so I guess so." The blonde laughs. "It'll be fine, though. We can always head to another bar if he doesn't take the hint."

They quickly run their hands through their hair, check their cleavage, adjust their skirts, and leave in as big a flourish as they arrived.

It's as good a time as any for me to do the same.

Maybe after I put on lip gloss.

I finally force myself to leave the bathroom, and take my time wandering back to the table. On the way, I spot Bryan at the bar. He's smiling, which makes me smile. This is so much better than seeing him mope over Heather.

But my heart sinks when I notice that he's leaning toward the blonde girl from the bathroom. Everything from her tight mouth to her crossed arms to the way she's backing away tells me that she isn't into him. Worse, whatever he's saying is making her angry.

And that's when I realize: The "foreign guy" she was talking about with the smile and the body and the accent is my brother.

Her friend and three guys are moving in closer and closer to them. And clearly, Bryan doesn't like whatever it is that they're saying to him. He shoves one guy. Another shoves Bryan against the bar.

"Hey!" the bartender yells.

Without even stopping to think, I run over, push through the small group, and grab Bryan's arm. "Let's go." I look into the eyes of the girl he was trying to chat up. "He's going to leave you alone now."

"I'm fine, Coley." Bryan tries to shrug me off. "Just having a little conversation here."

"No," the brunette says. "You're just being an asshole."

He rolls his eyes. "Sure. *I'm* an asshole because your friend can't take a compliment."

"Dude, walk away," says one of the guys. "She already said she's not interested."

"Please, Bryan," I say.

He doesn't make a move, so I grab on tightly and pull him away.

"*We* didn't need to go anywhere." Bryan raises his voice as I drag him back toward where we were sitting. "Who the fuck do they think they are anyway?"

I put out my hand when we reach our table. "Give me your wallet."

He reaches into his pocket and hands it over. I pass a handful of Canadian bills to Reece, who's looking up at us with his mouth open. So much for the worst of the night having already happened. "Can you take care of the bill?" I ask him. "I need to get Bryan out to the truck."

"Should I get our food to go or try to cancel the order?" Reece asks.

"Whatever you want," I say.

Reece sets the money on the table and stands. "Are you sure you don't need help?"

"We'll be fine," I say.

He slips me his keys. I wrap my arms around Bryan again and we stumble through the restaurant and outside, into the cold. He's still wearing his clunky snowboarding boots and dragging his feet, which isn't making this easy at all.

"God, I hate girls like that," Bryan grumbles.

And it seems to me that she hates "creepy creeps" like him, but I don't say it aloud.

At the truck, my hands shake more from anger than the cold as I unlock the doors, recline the passenger seat for Bryan, and then get into the backseat from the other side. Leaning over the driver's seat, I turn on the engine to get the heater going. The truck makes kind of a high-pitched grinding noise.

"What are you trying to do?" Bryan asks. "Burn out his starter?"

"Yes," I say, settling back onto the jump seat. "That was *exactly* my plan. I was thinking that I want to spend as much time as possible in this parking lot with you, so I might as well break Reece's truck."

He sighs. "Just don't turn the key for so long."

I don't answer.

Bryan crosses his arms over his eyes. "I can't even *talk* to some chick without almost getting my ass kicked," he says to the ceiling. "What the hell is wrong with me?"

"You're asking *me* this? Really? What's wrong with you is that you drank too much and totally embarrassed me in front of Reece and an entire restaurant full of people! Why'd you have to do that?"

"I don't know," he says bitterly.

"Figure it out. Next time, I'll leave you there."

"You probably should have." He makes a few quick sniffs as if he's trying not to cry. "I'm such a loser."

I want to stay mad at him—I *am* still mad—but no matter what, he's my brother. He needs for someone to be on his side and I'm all that he has. I reach forward and gently adjust his hat that's sliding off. "Reece is going to get us back to the house soon and we can forget this ever happened, okay?"

"I can't handle this, Coley." He lets out a ragged breath. "I really, really can't."

"You just need some sleep and you'll feel better," I say.

I think I sound pretty convincing, but I'm sure that neither of us believes a word that I'm saying.

CHAPTER 13

Back at the town house, Reece helps me drag Bryan out of the truck and into the foyer. "I've got him now," I say. "I'll come back up in a few minutes."

Reece nods and heads outside again to grab our takeout boxed dinners and Bryan's stuff. It was lucky for us that the greeter remembered Bryan had stored his backpack and snowboard at the coat-check station. Otherwise, we would have left it all behind.

Bryan grabs for the handrail and misses. "I can walk on my own," he says.

"Not very well." I hold on to his waist as he trips his way down the first couple of steps. "Slow down. Lean against me, okay?"

"I'm not as wasted as you think I am," he says into my hair.

Yeah, right.

We finally make it to the bottom of the staircase where

our stepdad almost collides with us. Even with Tony's lack of expression, I know that he knows Bryan's drunk, and he's not pleased about it.

"Oh, hi!" I say. "What's going on?"

Tony lifts up Emma's suitcase. "We've moved your sister to the pullout couch next to the boys' room. That way, your mom and I can check on her easier throughout the night."

"What about Reece?"

"I've put his things in the living room. We're all turning in early, so he won't be disturbed. I take it you're going to bed now too?"

I glance at my brother out of the corner of my eye. The wall and I are all that's holding him up. I don't want to admit to Tony that I wasn't able to eat yet, so I say, "Bryan is, I think. And I will pretty soon."

"Good."

With that, Tony steps around us and heads upstairs.

I help Bryan to his room and flip on the light. He crashes forward onto his unmade bed and lies there with his legs dangling over. "I hate it when you're pissed at me," he mumbles.

"Shhh." I grab his hat and toss it toward an open dresser drawer. "It's okay."

I untie his boots and yank them off, and then kneel on the mattress beside him. His arms and neck flop around so much as I pull his shirt over his head that I decide he can deal with his own pants later. "Come on. Get under the covers." I move to stand beside the bed and fluff his pillow. He crawls up. "Are you going to be sick?" I ask, tucking the blankets around him. "Do you need some water or aspirin or something?"

He doesn't respond, which is perfectly fine with me. With any luck, he'll be passed out until morning.

In the living room, the couch has already been converted and the cushions are piled against the wall. Reece is at the table, eating his barbecue chicken sandwich out of the box.

"I'm sorry," he says. "Your stepdad told me you'd gone to bed so I put yours in the fridge."

"What? It isn't even nine o'clock!" I grab my food from the kitchen and then take a seat next to him at the head of the table. "So that was an interesting night out," I say, putting on a smile. "Nonstop fun. That's what you get on vacation with me."

He smiles back. "So true."

I lift the lid on my container and poke some loose cabbage into a fish taco. "Bryan's whole harassing-a-girl-and-almost-getting-into-a-bar-fight thing was kind of exciting. I won't be forgetting that particular fun for a while."

"It's okay." Reece says it like he means it; like he has no doubt that my light tone is all an act.

I dig into my barely warm tacos and fries. I'm the one who mentioned Bryan, but I don't want to talk about him anymore; I don't even want to think about him. What I want is to go back to how things were earlier when Reece was holding my hand. And hugging me. And kissing me.

After a minute or two of us chewing, Reece clears his throat. "Coley, can I ask you something?"

I nod, even though I can tell by his voice that I'm not going to be excited to answer his question.

"What you said before," he says. "About your mom running away from New Zealand. Were you saying that your dad was abusive?"

After all the distractions with my brother tonight, I still didn't manage to escape this discussion. I can't blame Reece for asking, though. I'd ask too, if I were him. Sinking back against my chair, I say, "Yes, he was."

"So did he . . . hit her? And you and Bryan?"

I twist my hands. Alejandra is the only other person I've ever talked to about this and those discussions feel like they happened forever ago. "Maybe? I know he would beat up my mom, but I'm not sure if he did anything to Bryan and me or not. We don't talk about that kind of stuff. I've had nightmares for a long time, but they aren't actual memories, I don't think."

In my worst dream—the one I've had dozens and dozens of times, since before I can remember—I'm always running, trying to hide. It doesn't matter where I go or how many doors I lock, I'm never safe.

I start talking again, to keep from dwelling on this depressing stuff. "Did you ever have those *Wizard of Oz* nightmares? The angry tree that throws apples? The witch's feet that shrivel up underneath the house? Flying monkeys? That's some super scary stuff, am I right?"

Reece doesn't crack a smile. Instead, he seems to be studying me, trying to figure me out. "I hate thinking that anyone would hurt you," he says, scooting his chair closer to mine. "And that it would be so bad that you still have nightmares."

I look into his eyes. "*Don't* think about it. I never do. Unlike my brother, I'm fine."

He nods slowly, still looking doubtful.

"Reece, I promise you. I don't remember it at all. And I should never have brought it up," I say, smiling big, "because you came here for a good time, and this is *so* the opposite."

"I'm glad you told me, though." He touches my arm. "And I'm especially glad that your mom got you guys away."

"Me too."

I don't know what else to say. It happened, Bryan's still

messed up all these years later, and I have no idea how I can help him. Maybe no one can help him.

No. I shouldn't think like that. I really, really shouldn't.

I crumple my napkin and snap my container shut. Reece does the same, and we sit, looking at each other. The silence doesn't start out uncomfortable, but the longer it goes on, the more curious I become about what he's thinking. What does he want to happen next?

I want to be close to him. I want him to kiss me again. Most of all, I want him to tell me what he's feeling, even if the words have to come from a song.

"Do you want to watch TV or something?" I ask.

"Yeah," he says quickly.

We get up together and throw our containers away. He takes my hand and leads me out of the kitchen, into the living room, and onto his bed.

Reece Kinsey and I.

Are on a bed.

Together.

Sitting between Sterling the Giraffe and me, Reece leans back against the pillows and stretches his legs out, like it's no big deal, like we've done this every day of our lives. "What should we watch?"

I glance at the black TV screen, and then back at him. "Um. I don't know."

It's the best I can come up with under these circumstances.

Neither of us makes a move toward grabbing the remote, though. Instead, he puts his arm around me and pulls me close. I snuggle in until my head's on his shoulder and my hand is across his chest.

We stay like this for five years or maybe five minutes and my heart thuds like crazy for every single second and it *is* a big deal because I can feel his heart doing the same thing.

"I like this show," Reece says by my ear. "It's one of my favorites."

I giggle and sit up a little, positioning my face within inches of his. "Hey, do you remember that time when we were in a hot tub and your hand was trying to get all frisky with my hand?"

"Is that what it was trying to do?" he asks, smiling.

"I think so." I run my fingers over his. "And then you came up with the wacky idea to go out in the snow and my little brothers locked us outside?"

"Hmm. Yeah. I remember all of this pretty well since it was, like, two hours ago?"

"Do you still think it's the best day ever?"

He nods and I move closer and he turns his body toward mine and we're kissing again and I'm still not sure if I'm doing it right, but he *definitely* is and I don't care where we are right now because only *this* matters—only Reece, who smells like fabric softener and soap and chlorine, whose hands are on my back and in my hair.

"I had it planned," he says, pulling away a century before I'm ready for him to, "that if I ever got the chance to kiss you, I'd quote 'Brown Eyed Girl' afterward."

"But you didn't."

He tilts his head. "Well. I don't want to assume anything."

Wasn't I clear when we were texting last night? And all day today? And especially *just now* when we were kissing? Does he really need for me to say it?

Maybe he does.

I move my face close again and stare into his eyes. "Reece, I'm your brown-eyed girl. If you're all right with that?"

"I'm very all right with it."

It is official now. Reece is my boyfriend!

"Are there any green-eyed boy songs?" I ask.

"Actually, Dolly Parton has one." He grins. "But before you say that I know every single song in the world, you should know that I looked it up. For in case you knew it."

I laugh. "So you were assuming *something*, it sounds like."

"Nope. Just hoping."

Still smiling, I move back in to kiss him again, but then I hear Tony's voice. "Coley! I thought you said you were going to bed."

"Oh!" I sit up straight and slide away from Reece in a hurry. "I am." I look over my shoulder at Tony, standing on the upper staircase in his bathrobe. "I mean, I'm about to. I'm just not very tired, really."

"Tired or not, your mother wants you in your room."

"Okay. I'll go in a few minutes."

"You'll go now."

I hold in a sigh. "See you in the morning," I say to Reece, giving his hand a quick squeeze.

He lifts the giraffe and touches her to my cheek as if she's kissing me. "See you then."

CHAPTER 14

I'm lying alone in the middle of this huge bed, tracing my fingers over my giraffe pendant still clasped around my neck. I feel so different from who I was yesterday. From who I was a few hours ago, even. I'm Reece's girlfriend now. I've experienced his soap and fabric softener scent way up close, his cinnamon kisses, the smoothness of his face. Yesterday, I liked him—a lot. But tonight, my head has these amazing tingles from thinking his name. His name!

Smiling in the darkness, I say it over and over in my mind: *Reece, Reece, Reece, Reece, Reece.*

I whisper it, "Reece, Reece, Reece, Reece, Reece."

My door opens. Closes again.

For a split second, I wonder if maybe it's Reece.

But it isn't. I know it isn't.

I squeeze my eyes shut as he climbs under the covers, slides close to me, and turns me over so that we're lying facing each other. I'm a rag doll, silently breathing in cologne and beer.

Rubbing one hand up and down my back, Bryan whispers, "Baby, I need you so bad right now."

His lips crash into mine: once, twice, three times.

My eyelids fly open. He's never kissed me before. Not on the mouth.

Bryan's eyes are closed. "I love you," he says, pulling me to him. "I love you so fucking much it kills me."

I don't know where he thinks he is or who he thinks he's with, but it isn't here and it isn't me. With my heart beating out of control, I try to push away, but he tugs me back. I squirm in his arms.

"No, don't go!" He starts to cry. His fingers tangle in my hair and he squeezes me so tightly to his chest that I can't move or take any but the shallowest breaths. His tears get all over my face, and I can't wipe them away because both of my arms are pinned between us. "Don't leave me, Coley," he says, sobbing. "Please. Promise me you won't ever leave. *Promise.*"

So he does know who I am. Somehow, that makes me feel better and worse at the same time. I want to cry with him, but I'm feeling too numb, too confused, too guilty. I can't tell him what he wants to hear—I can't say anything because that would mean that this is real—but I stop fighting. I lie perfectly still in his hold.

He lets out a loud breath and loosens his grip. His hands massage my back again, gentler this time. This part. This is exactly how it starts, how it's started since I was seven and he was eleven. Backrubs that turn into front rubs that turn into everything-else rubs. I don't have it in me to do anything except let it happen.

Over his shoulder, the glowing red numbers on the alarm clock switch from 11:10 to 11:11. I close my eyes and make a wish.

I wish I were with Reece. I wish that he had been on his pullout bed and couldn't sleep. He decided that he couldn't take it anymore; he had to be with me. So he snuck downstairs and let himself into my room. Now he's here. Reece is in my bed, caressing my back . . . my shoulders . . . my sides . . . my stomach . . . my breasts . . .

It's perfect. This is all very natural, being touched by Reece. It's the sort of thing that a normal girl would totally want the guy she likes to do to her.

Keeping my eyes shut, I stroke his face and pretend that the stubble and dampness on his cheeks don't exist.

Reece, Reece, Reece, Reece, Reece.

His lips keep hitting mine and just once—just for a second or two—I kiss him back.

Reece, Reece, Reece, Reece, Reece.

He takes off my pajamas and I don't help him, but I don't *not* help, either. The blankets keep shifting and the air is cold and I'm shivering in socks and panties. He undresses himself completely and we're skin on skin and lips on skin and lips on lips and it's happening so quickly and he rolls me onto my back and lowers himself over me and he's moving on me, against me, and my underwear is the only thing between us, the only thing keeping him *out* of me and my heart is pounding and he's going faster and faster and faster and hot pulsing takes over my body and he eases back and grabs my hand and uses it how he wants it, how he needs it, until finally—*finally* he collapses, panting and crushing me into the mattress.

I'm a shaking mess. It's as if every inch of me is covered in Bryan. My tears mix with his from earlier, stream across my temples, fall into my hair and ears.

He catches his breath. "Coley, do you love me?"

I kind of hate him for asking the question, but after a few seconds, I whisper, "Yes."

Because, in spite of everything, it's the truth.

CHAPTER 15

Bryan's gone and I'm still shivering, but I can't bring myself to cover up or get dressed—not when I'm all sticky like this. I dig around the blankets until I find my pajamas and then take them with me as I creep through the dark to the bathroom.

Inside, I lock the door and turn on the light. I can't see anything at first as my pupils adjust, but then I'm startled by the messy hair, red eyes, and tear-streaked cheeks of the mostly naked person blinking back at me in the mirror.

Disgusting. I am a disgusting girl who lets her brother put his mouth and hands on her wherever he wants, whenever he wants. A girl who *just laid there* while he used her to get off. A girl who didn't want this—did she?—but whose underwear tells a different story.

I slap my face as hard as I can. It hurts, but not enough. I make a fist and slam it into my cheekbone. This time, tears pour from my eyes and drip onto my chest and stomach. My hand and cheek throb in sync.

I can't stand to look at myself for another second, so I flip the light switch. In the blackness again, I peel off my socks and underwear and feel my way into the shower. The water is an icy blast that gradually turns to scalding. I lather, scrub, and rinse my skin over and over, pausing only to yank the lever handle from too hot to too cold and back again.

It doesn't help.

CHAPTER 16

I can't go back to my room. I won't. I'll be quiet. I'll head upstairs. I'll sleep with Emma. Or on the floor. Or anywhere. *Any*where. I don't care where.

I don't care.

With my towel still wrapped around my hair, I make my way up the first and second staircases as silently as I can. A living room lamp is on and Reece is sitting up in bed with his computer on his lap and the stuffed giraffe that "kissed" me good night still propped up on the pillow beside him.

"Hey! Is it morning already?" he asks.

"No. I . . . got thirsty," I say, turning and rushing into the kitchen.

I am the worst girlfriend *in the world*. Not even two hours into us making things official, I've already betrayed him in the worst way. I yank a water pitcher from the fridge and, out of the corner of my eye, see him making his way in and opening and closing cupboards. When he finds the glasses, he pulls two out.

"You can't sleep either, I take it?" he asks, setting them in front of me.

"No." I pour the water and push a glass his way without looking at him.

"I have to say, I'm glad." There's a smile in his voice. "Because I would have hated to miss seeing you with that twirled towel on your head."

I cover my face with one hand. "Don't, okay? I look awful."

"What? That's crazy!"

I'm crazy. And awful. I'm a crazy, awful person and I can't . . . breathe.

I stare at our bare feet, at the lines on the tile flooring, at the three Cheerios someone must have spilled this morning, at anything and everything that helps me avoid Reece's gaze.

I can't breathe. I can't breathe. I can't breathe.

"Hey, are you okay?" Reece asks.

I shake my head so hard that the towel comes loose, slides down my face, and lands in a pile on the floor. My shoulders sink and my knees give way, and an instant before I hit the floor, he lunges forward and catches me under my arms. He lifts and pulls me against him. "What's wrong? Did you get a head rush?"

I'm gasping and gasping and gasping, but I can't get enough air. My arms are around Reece's waist, but it's only his firm hands on my back that are keeping me from crumbling onto the towel and the tiles and the Cheerios.

"Let's sit you down," he says.

I let him help me over to his bed. He moves his computer to the coffee table while I crawl under the blankets, squeeze my eyes shut, and make myself as small as possible.

Breathe, breathe, breathe, breathe.

"You feel sick?" he says as he sits beside me.

The sickest.

"No," I say, into the pillow.

"Did you have a bad dream?"

A dream. Yes. That's what it was. I had another horrible, horrible nightmare.

I nod.

"What we were talking about earlier must have triggered it. I'm really sorry, Coley."

I open my eyes. His mouth is turned down and his forehead is lined; he seems to think that he's to blame for this—all because he asked me those questions about my father.

Now I'm sorry.

I am so, so sorry.

A sob escapes my lips and Reece scoots closer. I throw my arms around him, rest my face against his chest.

"It's okay," he says, rubbing my back as I cry. "You're okay."

He's so wrong and he has no idea. It's totally unfair for me to put him through this; I know that it is. Still, I keep holding on. I keep soaking his shirt with my tears. I can't make myself stop.

I'm drifting in and out of sleep. I'm in Reece's arms. I'm pinned beneath Bryan. I'm curled up alone. The locks are broken always, always broken. The door won't stay shut. This isn't safe. I'm not safe.

Someone strokes my hair. *Who?*

"I'm still here, Coley," Reece whispers.

Reece. He's here, he's here, he's here.

But he isn't really. I'm alone with the giraffe. I can feel it.

I squint in the lamp light, close my eyes again.

My head pounds.

My cheek pulsates.

I hear quiet, terse voices from somewhere across the room.

Tony: ". . . *not* grasping why you'd think this would be okay!"

Reece: "I'm sorry. I swear to you, it isn't what it looks like. Coley had a bad dream and—"

Tony: "Really? I didn't know she still had those. She hasn't mentioned nightmares for years."

Reece: "She was freaked and I didn't think she should be alone. I didn't know what else to do."

. . .

Tony: "All right. Well, you need to get some sleep. You've got another long drive tomorrow. Obviously, her room's empty, so why don't you head down there?"

. . .

Reece: "I kind of—I don't want to leave her, you know? If she wakes up and I'm not here—"

Tony: "I'll keep an eye on her."

. . .

. . .

Reece: "Well. Okay."

. . .

Tony: "Good night, then."

. . .

. . .

. . .

Someone kisses my forehead.

. . .

. . .

. . .

. . .

I wrap my arms around Sterling.

. . .

. . .

. . .

. . .

. . .

We float away.

CHAPTER 17

Layers of concealer, foundation, powder, and blush aren't hiding the mark on my cheek, none of the hairstyles I've attempted will stay in place to cover it, and a bandage would only make my family ask more questions. I'm out of options. I'm out of patience.

There's a knock on the door and my mother calls out, "Nicole, we need to talk!"

I'm out of time.

Flipping my hair in front of half of my face, I pull the bathroom door open.

Mom is in the hall with her arms crossed in front of her. "Tony tells me you were upstairs with Reece after being told *twice* to go to bed last night?"

There's an edge to her voice. I don't know what I expected, but seriously, couldn't Tony have at least tried to sell her on Reece's perfectly legitimate-sounding, bad-dream explanation?

"It isn't what you're thinking," I tell her.

"Oh, I think it's *exactly* what I'm thinking." Her voice is rising with every syllable. "I can't believe that you would be so disrespectful and inappropriate and, oh my God, Nicole!"

As always, she sees threats where there are none and misses what's real.

Frustration ripples through me. "Nothing happened, Mom. I promise."

She shakes her head. "I knew I shouldn't have let that kid come. I should have trusted my gut."

"You aren't listening to me! We didn't do anything, so get over it."

She opens her mouth, but no words come and we stand there, glaring at each other. Finally, she speaks in a quiet voice, "I think the girl who snuck out of her room to be with a boy last night needs to watch how she speaks to her mother. And you'd better believe that after he's gone, we're going to be having a long discussion about your behavior." She turns away and shouts on her way up the steps, "Bry-yan! Breakfast is getting co-old!"

I can't leave Reece up there to deal with my mom without me, so I give myself one last glance in the mirror, adjust my hair, and start after her.

Bryan's door flies open and we reach the stairs at the

same moment. He's a stubble-faced, messy-haired wreck in jeans and a T-shirt that look like they've been smashed under a couch cushion for a month. We both hesitate, and then he waves for me to go first. I run full speed to the top.

Upstairs, everyone's eating. Emma's on the couch with her foot propped up, Tony, Jacob, Zach, and Reece are at the table, and Mom is on a barstool at the island. Bryan and I maneuver around each other in the kitchen, grabbing plates, scooping up eggs and fruit and potatoes and bacon, pouring juice.

Over the years, we've had dozens of mornings after, but this one is different. Because of Reece, but mostly, because of Bryan.

Because of how he was last night.

Because he spoke while he was with me.

Because he kissed me on the lips.

And all the rest of it. Everything he did.

He'd never done any of those things to me before. He'd always let me sleep—or pretend to be asleep—while he touched me. But last night he made sure I was awake. He made it so that everything *he* was doing, *we* were doing.

Bryan takes a seat on the stool next to Mom and I make my way to the table. There's worry on Reece's face when he looks up at me, but his lips are upturned. I can tell that he still likes me, he still wants to be with me. It's so much more than I'm worthy of. I force myself to smile back.

"How are you this morning?" Tony asks me as I settle in between him and Reece.

I'm going to live through this. Somehow. I'll put it out of my mind. I'll fool myself into believing it never happened, that it was a bad dream. Because, truly, how *could* it have happened? Bryan's my brother. It doesn't even make sense.

"I'm embarrassed about the nightmare I had." My voice sounds surprising calm. "But I'm feeling much better now. Thank you for asking."

"That's good to hear." Tony goes back to his paper.

For the next couple of minutes, the only sounds are my heart hammering in my ears, silverware scraping plates, and Jacob's loud gulping.

I can feel Reece watching me, but I can't keep my eyes off Bryan. Bryan squeezing ketchup onto his potatoes. Bryan chewing, swallowing, chewing, swallowing. Bryan catching me looking. Bryan's eyes asking, "What's up?" even though we both know that he knows.

Or maybe . . . he doesn't know. Maybe he was so drunk that he had no idea what he was doing.

If Bryan has no recollection of last night . . .

If I was pretending to be with Reece . . .

If, in our minds, neither of us were truly there . . .

It couldn't have happened. It *didn't*.

Across from me with a mouthful of eggs, Jacob asks, "Hey, Coley. What happened to your face? You have a bruise on it or something."

"Oops." I touch my cheek absently, as if I didn't spend half an hour trying to cover it up. "I guess I must have hit it on the chair lift when I fell getting off yesterday."

Jacob's jaw drops and so does a tiny piece of egg onto his plate. So gross.

"You fell off the lift?" he asks. "For reals?"

"Jacob," Tony says, "don't act like it's never happened to you."

Mom speaks for the first time since Bryan and I came upstairs. "Obviously, everyone was not their most coordinated yesterday. Next trip, I think we need to remember to take more days off for simple relaxation. Who's with me?"

Tony lets out a growl. "Dawn—"

"I'm not *blaming*," she interrupts, putting one hand up. "I'm just saying."

Reece's worried face is back again. "Coley, I am so sorry. That looks like it hurts, too."

It does, but not as much as I deserve after managing to make Reece feel responsible for yet another thing that had nothing to do with him.

"I'm fine," I insist. "And it isn't your fault."

"Of course, it is. If I hadn't knocked you over—"

"Whoa!" Jacob looks back and forth between us. "Is that kinda like when Anakin lost control and killed Padme?"

He mimes being strangled by the Force and adds a choking sound-effect.

Tony is watching Reece and me, obviously waiting for one of us to explain Reece's apology now that Jacob made it sound so violent.

"It was nothing like Anakin," I say. "Reece lost control of his snowboard, not his emotions. I'm totally fine."

"Are you *sure*?" Reece asks.

"Very sure."

"And for the billionth time," Emma calls out from the couch, "Anakin didn't kill Padme!"

Zach chimes in. "If he *had*, it would have made more sense than how they did it in the movie. But . . . we shouldn't talk about it in front of Reece."

"Oh, sorry," Jacob says to Reece. "I forgot you said that you haven't even seen the ones with Anakin and Padme."

"You haven't?" Tony asks, grinning. "Do we have a purist among us?"

I glance at Bryan without even thinking about it—like I do whenever Tony geeks out. Sure enough, my brother is rolling his eyes at me. I look away.

"Not a purist," Reece says. "I just haven't gotten around to watching them. I'd like to, though."

Jacob says, "Can we have a *Star Wars* marathon someday at our house for Reece?"

"We'll see," Mom mutters.

But Tony says, "Sure. And I can show you my vinyls, too, while you're over. I've got jazz. I've got classical. I've got it all."

"That sounds cool," Reece says, nodding.

I have no idea what I missed while I was showering and getting ready, but everything's backward here: Tony's being nice to Reece, Mom's mad at everyone, and I don't want to look at my brother.

"I'm going to pack now," I say, pushing my chair out.

Downstairs, I throw all my bathroom stuff into my small bag. I head to the bedroom and strip off all the bedding for house-keeping. I set my suitcases open on the bed. The sooner I finish packing, the sooner I can escape this place for good.

I pull clothes from the drawers, the closet, the floor and throw them in my suitcase. I toss shoes, books, magazines into the mix. Whatever I see, I grab. Faster, faster, faster.

I hear someone coming down the stairs and then Bryan's voice behind me. "Hey."

My chest constricts. "What?" I ask, without turning, without slowing down.

"Look, I wanted to tell you, C. I'm really sorry."

My arms fall to my sides and my shoulders sink. I can't look at him. I don't want to talk about it. Only once has he ever admitted to anything out loud. It was during a tickle fight when I was thirteen and he was seventeen. I kept shrieking and panting while he was holding me down and he made some joke about me having an orgasm. When I asked what that meant, he said, "Trust me, you know."

Later, I looked up the definition and he was right; I'd known for quite a while.

Bryan speaks again. "The way I was acting at the restaurant was so out of line. You should never have had to deal with that. I'm going to make it up to you. I swear."

I turn slowly and stare at him, blinking, blinking, blinking to keep the moisture in my eyes from forming into real tears. His apology is for what he did *at the restaurant*?

He looks at the carpet. "So. I guess you're riding back today with Reece?"

A tear trickles down my cheek. Then another. I swipe them away with the back of my hand. "I doubt it. Mom's mad—"

"Yeah, I heard her. Just get your permission letter out of

my car, and you guys leave when I leave. She isn't going to cause a scene in front of him."

Bryan meets my gaze and we study each other for a long moment before he goes back to watching the floor. He remembers everything; I'm sure of it now. But why does he want me to go with Reece? To help "make it up to" me? Or because he doesn't want to be around me any more than I want to be around him?

He doesn't give an explanation. He doesn't give me anything. He just goes to his room with his head still down.

I push my door shut and lean against it, ruining my makeup as I sob quietly into my hands.

CHAPTER 18

About five hours before the scheduled start of the Crowne family's annual New Year's Eve party, a cosmetics-counter lady at the mall is painting lipstick stripes on the back of my hand. Long ago, Alejandra and I learned the hard way that makeup tested on our hands doesn't always look the same on our faces, but this woman seems too distracted by all the customers gathered around her booth to actually let me take the time to try any on my lips.

"All of these work with your skin tone," she says in a rush. "The Stellar Plum will be especially nice."

I'm unconvinced; I already told her that what I'm looking for is something to go with the red dress that I'm wearing tonight.

A girl's voice calls out from behind me. "Coley Sterling, is it really you?"

I turn, and Ming is stepping around people. Her hair is

pulled back in a ponytail that shows off her amethyst earrings from Xander and she has on a huge smile.

I wave at her, and then say to the saleswoman across the counter, "I'm going to have to think about this."

She hands me a tissue without a word, and I quickly wipe off my hand, step aside for the next customer, and head over to Ming who's waiting near a perfume case.

"What a surprise, seeing you here," I say, returning her smile. "You'd think we planned it or something."

She grips my arm as I get close. "Oh, my *gosh*, Coley!"

"Ouch!"

"Sorry." She loosens her hold. "It's just that I've been dying to talk to you about Xander and me. How much time do you have?"

I've been grounded for the past five days—ever since Reece dropped me off after the Whistler trip—so I haven't been able to go anywhere or hang out with anyone. My life lately has been all about homework, watching TV with the triplets, and sending thousands of texts. This last-minute mall trip with Mom before the big party tonight is the first time she's allowed me to step outside of the house, even though I'm not exactly speaking to her.

"I have only as long as it will take for my mom to get her hair and eyebrows done," I say. "Tell me about you and Xander."

"Okay. We"—Ming lowers her voice to a near-whisper—
"did it."

"It?" I ask.

She nods. *"It."*

I don't know how to respond. The only time I've ever had
a friend confide in me about this type of thing—aside from
Truth or Dare—was Alejandra at that Saturday dance practice
in October.

"Aren't you going to say something?" Ming asks.

"Of course. Just not exactly right *here.*" I look around
and pull her to the escalator. We run to the top and rush into
the ladies' lounge. Luckily, the sofa is free. "So was *it* something you hadn't done before?" I ask as we throw ourselves
down.

"Neither of us had," she says. "But now we have!"

"Yay!" We bounce up and down on the couch together,
until I realize what we're doing. "Okay, this is just wrong."

"What? This?" She gets up on her knees and bounces
faster and harder, grinning while I'm jostled all over the
cushions and my legs hit against my bag on the floor. "For
the past eight days, this is exactly what I've wanted to do,"
she says. "Jump on a couch and yell, 'My boyfriend and I
had sex!'"

"Will! You! Stop!" I shriek, unable to hold in my laughter.

It amazes me how genuinely happy she is about this. Nothing at all like how Alejandra was.

"Okay, okay." Ming puts her feet back down and folds her hands over her lap. "In case you wondered, he didn't actually go that fast. Not until the final seconds, I mean."

"Ming!"

She bursts out laughing, and I can't help joining in, even though my face is getting hotter and hotter, thinking about the intensity of "the final seconds."

"I seriously don't need to hear those details," I say.

"You don't? Not even, like, positions or how long it lasted—"

"No!"

"Wow. You're letting me off easy." Her voice is tinged with disappointment. "I went to a movie with Dia and Kimber, and they pretty much wanted me to draw a diagram to scale. I didn't, though, because there was no way I was going to boink and tell to *them*."

Ming wants me to be excited and interested. She seems to need for me to be. "Okay," I say, faking it a little. "Give me one detail. Was it romantic like in a movie or was it embarrassing?"

She smiles. "Both. Romantic because it was with him. Embarrassing because of everything else about it. Just the first time, though."

My phone chimes with a new text, but I ignore it. There's no way my mom could be looking for me already. She isn't big on texting anyway; she'll call when she's ready. "There was more than one time?"

Ming nods. "The night after Christmas and again two days ago."

The door between the lounge and the bathroom opens and a woman and a little girl come out together. Ming and I pause our conversation until they pass through. "And the second time was better?" I ask.

"Yes!" She smiles big. "Way, way, way better."

"Does that mean that you . . . ?"

I trail off, not sure of the best way to phrase it.

"That I *what*?" She tilts her head "Ohhh. You're wondering about the Big O?"

Now my face feels like it's on fire. "No. I'm wondering about Kimber and Dia. How are they? What movie did you see?"

"Let me try to remember," she says, tapping her cheek with her fingertip. "Oh, yeah. It was that new one called 'No, I didn't have an orgasm, but thank you for asking.'"

I didn't actually ask, but she guessed correctly what I was wondering about. *Why* would I wonder about that? "I'm sorry. That was way too nosy, wasn't it?"

She shakes her head. "I don't mind with you. But there's a lot that I didn't want to tell Dia and Kimber, so this all has to stay between us, okay?"

"Okay," I say cautiously.

She lets out a loud breath. "So you know how people always say that your first time is all pain and gore?"

I nod, even though I've never actually heard it described in quite that way.

"So I was prepared," Ming says. "But what no one ever told me about is, you know, the *parts* and the fact that they don't just slip into place. There's, like, angles to work out. We couldn't, um, get it in. And we both wanted to die of embarrassment. At one point, we looked at each other and started laughing hysterically because there was nothing else to do."

I've never heard of this angle thing, either. "Obviously, you figured it out, though."

Ming's phone beeps. "Eventually," she says. "The second time was way, way, way better because we had a better idea what to do." She takes her phone out and looks at the screen. "And look! A text from my hot boyfriend. He and Brody are on their way to the food court. Do you still have time?"

I check my phone to make sure. Just as I suspected, the text from a couple of minutes ago wasn't from Mom.

Piper: Can you do me a super HUGE favor and help me put my hair up before the party? Pleeeeeease?

"I still have time," I tell Ming.

She types back to Xander, and I send a quick response to let Piper know that I'll be there an hour early to style her hair.

As we head out of the lounge, Ming says, "They're at the other end of the mall, so I told Xander we'll find a table and he and Brody can meet us there."

"Oh, great. It just occurred to me that I'm now going to have to see your boyfriend after the things I've heard."

She laughs and we step onto the escalator behind a big family. "That's how *I* felt about seeing him after the first time. I got over it, though." She lowers her voice. "I've been teasing him that we should have watched porn first so that we wouldn't have been so clueless."

"Too much information!" I cover my ears. "Between your and Alejandra's horror stories, I'm not sure that I ever want to . . . *you know.*"

"It won't be like that if your first time's with Reece," Ming says. "But speaking of Alejandra—has it ever occurred to you that maybe she wasn't into that guy? That she only went out with him to make you jealous?"

I think back to this past summer at camp, to the night that Derrick first kissed Alejandra. When she came back to our room and told me about it afterward, she'd seemed worried about how I was going to take the news, but mostly she'd seemed excited that he felt the same way about her that she felt about him.

"Alejandra was totally in love with Derrick," I say as we reach the main level and head toward the mall corridor. "Her decision to go out with him had nothing to do with me."

Ming shrugs. "You know her a lot better than I do. But, I mean, how dramatic is *she*? Breaking up with someone she supposedly loved because her first time wasn't as good as she wanted it to be? I could never have done that to Xander."

"Maybe Derrick didn't watch porn either, and Alejandra just took it more personally than you did?"

She gives me a small push, and I laugh as if I really don't care. Honestly, though, this conversation with Ming has made me more confused than ever about why Alejandra did what she did.

At the food court, Ming and I find an empty table for four and sit across from each other. "When's Reece coming back from Portland?" she asks.

"Not until Sunday night. Just in time to go back to school on Monday."

She chews her fingernail. "You won't tell him all that stuff I told you, right?"

"About you and Xander? Of course not."

"And . . . you won't tell Xander?"

I burst out laughing at that. "I can't imagine any circumstance ever that would get your boyfriend and me talking about *that*."

"But if it came up somehow, you'd keep quiet? I don't want to embarrass him."

"My lips are sealed forever and ever. I promise."

"Promise what?" Xander asks.

"Oh!" Ming yelps. "You're here!"

"I thought you were expecting me?" he says, smiling down at her. "Or did someone else send me that text?"

Brody takes the seat next to me and immediately pulls out his phone, while Ming grabs Xander's hand and has him sit beside her. She bulges her eyes at me as if to ask if I think they heard anything. I don't think so, but I keep my expression blank so that it won't be obvious that we're attempting to have a telepathic conversation.

"What?" Xander asks. "What's going on?"

"Nothing!" Ming smiles at him.

"You're both looking at me weird." He rubs the end of his nose. "Don't tell me I have a booger hanging out."

"You don't." Ming leans in and gives him a quick kiss. Then she looks at me again. "Hey, Coley!" she says in an overly chipper voice that's sure to keep Xander suspicious. "Are you going to Brody's party on Friday after the basketball game?"

"I hadn't heard about it," I say.

"That's because I'm not having a party," Brody says, without looking up from his phone.

"Dude, seriously," Xander says.

"I'm *not*."

"Okay, fine," Xander says. "But one of your sisters is having a party at the house where you also happen to live. It's pretty much the same thing."

"You should see if you can spend the night with me that night," Ming says to me. "And then we'll all go to the kegger that Brody *isn't* having."

I've never been to a "kegger." I've actually never been to any party that didn't involve movies, ice cream, and sleeping bags on my teammates' floors, but I say, "I'll ask."

"Hey, Brode," Xander says, "I figured out a way to get Taku and Seth and Rosetta to come. We could do something with the band that night. Play a little show downstairs maybe?"

"No way," Brody says, setting his phone on the table. "I don't want people in my studio."

"You have a studio?" I ask.

Brody nods.

"That's where we practice every day and where I keep my drums," Xander says.

"I want to play your drums!" Ming says.

Xander looks at Brody. "Can I at least take Ming and Coley down that night, so they can check it out?"

"And Coley's boyfriend," Ming says.

"Fine," Brody says. "Ming, Coley, and Noah. No one else. I'm serious, Xander."

"Noah?" I ask.

Ming laughs. "Her boyfriend is Reece, not Noah."

"Oh." Brody shrugs. "Did you guys break up or something?"

"We're just friends," I say. "Noah's been, like, my best guy friend since kindergarten."

"Oh," Brody says again.

"You know what I just realized?" Ming says. "It's going to be crazy when we get back to school and people find out you're with Reece. Everyone's going to think you dumped Noah for him and there will be drama and rumors all over the place!"

I say, "I doubt people pay that much attention to Noah and me to even care."

"Brody obviously does," she says.

"Not *really*." Brody's cheeks redden. He looks around and stands up. "I'm getting a burrito."

Ming scrunches up her face as he walks away.

"I guess I'll go see what his deal is," Xander says. "Do you want anything?"

"Cinnabon?" Ming suggests.

"You got it."

Xander goes after Brody, and Ming shakes her head. "I swear. The guys Xander hangs out with are so *moody*. Aren't you glad we set you up with his only non-emo friend?"

I've always suspected that Ming and Xander had purposely been trying to get Reece and me together, but this is the first time she's ever confessed it to me.

"You know what?" I say, smiling at her. "I *am* glad."

CHAPTER 19

An hour into the Crowne's New Year's Eve party, Piper and I are surrounded by the Law Offices of Crowne and DeLuca's attorneys and admin staff, everyone's significant others, and a few clients and fellow country club members. I don't know how much longer I can take this—my new heels are killing me. The fact that Bryan isn't here yet is clearly killing Piper.

I'm sure that he'll show up eventually—my mom's late too, and they're coming together—but I don't bother reassuring Piper. She hasn't admitted to me that her sapphire blue dress and the pretty chignon that I pinned up for her are all for *him*, but I know it's true. Whether or not he'll care is the real question.

Well, that, and whether he'll talk to me. Bryan's been gone a lot since we got back from Whistler, hanging out with friends from high school while I've been trapped at home. I know that he's avoiding me on purpose, and part of me is *almost* okay with it. I haven't been sleeping much, though, wondering every night if he's going to change his mind.

"I still can't believe Alejandra," Piper says, going back to her default topic of the night. "We start school again in two days so she can't avoid us forever."

Alejandra hasn't responded to even one of Piper's texts or calls about the Starbucks meeting that we were trying to set up for the other day. Not that it would have mattered anyway, since Mom wouldn't have let me go.

"You aren't the one she's avoiding," I say. "So don't take it personally."

"I'm *not*," Piper says, even though it's obvious by how she keeps bringing it up that she totally is. "The real problem is that Coach isn't going to put up with it anymore," she says. "And it's going to end up hurting you the most. I mean, let's face it. You and Alejandra are the two best sophomore dancers on the team, but only *you* are captain material."

Instantly and unexpectedly, I'm on the defensive. "Why would you say that? She's a better dancer than most of the seniors even, her choreography's amazing, and—"

"And she doesn't have what it takes to be a leader, Coley. You do." Piper sips from her glass of sparkling punch. "I feel like if you fix things with her, you can turn this around and prove to Coach and the rest of the team that you're right for the job. By the end of the school year, when it's time to vote, everyone will have forgotten that they had doubts about you."

I fall silent and let her words soak in. Alejandra and I used to talk about it so much. How we'd both be captains senior year. How, if we worked hard enough this year, maybe we'd be picked as juniors, too. I want it, with or without Alejandra. I didn't realize until now that the "with Alejandra" part still mattered to me.

Noah wanders back into the room, playing with his tie. "Is there anything more ridiculous than dressing up to hang out in my own house?" he asks, standing beside me.

"Be quiet," Piper says, looking around at all the nearby adults, who happen to be drinking, chatting, laughing, and *not* paying attention to the three teenagers in their midst.

Why Tony and Mr. Crowne think it's important that we come to this annual event is beyond me. Secretly I envy the triplets, who are spending New Year's Eve at our house with a babysitter like Bryan, Piper, Noah, and I used to do when we were younger. Of course, back then we always wished we were here so we'd have a better view of the fireworks over the lake.

Noah lowers his voice. "I decided to go commando in secret protest. Now, with the chafing, it's my dick that's protesting."

I giggle.

Piper frowns at both of us. "That's disgusting. I don't want to hear about your non-underwear habits."

"I wouldn't say that free balling is a *habit* of mine." A grin spreads across Noah's face. "But I could maybe turn it into one. I just have to build up some calluses."

Piper shakes her head.

I cover my smile with my fingers, and Noah turns his attention to me. "Coley, is it the lighting in here, or did someone punch you?"

"*I* did," I say, testing out how the words sound.

My bruise is still dark. With this and my big, crusty scab from my curling iron—covered at the moment by the chiffon wrap that I'm refusing to take off—I'm looking somewhat less than awesome from the neck up.

Noah's eyes widen. "You punched your own face?"

So I sound completely crazy then.

"Like I'm that hardcore," I say. "It was more of a cheek-meets-chairlift kind of a deal." I skim my hand down the side of my satin dress. "Too bad purple clashes with red."

"Yeah, you sure didn't plan that very well," Noah says.

Just then Piper stands up straighter and watches the now-open front door. I follow her gaze to where my mother is breezing through in a black, sequined dress. Bryan's right behind her. He looks halfway decent for a change; he even shaved.

"Sorry, I'm late!" Mom announces.

"Mrs. DeLuca," Noah says, "if you were on time, you wouldn't be you."

He's teasing her, but it's the truth, too.

Noah steps forward to take Mom's wrap and clutch, while my brother rushes past Piper and me to the champagne fountain.

Like Piper, I'm frozen in this spot, watching Bryan's every move. I used to be good at making myself forget about the things that happened between us. Now I feel like I'm suffocating from having to be in the same room with him.

Noah comes back from putting Mom's stuff away at the same time that Bryan makes his way over.

"How's it going?" Bryan asks.

His question doesn't seem to have been directed at anyone in particular, but he's looking my way for what might be the first time all week.

"We're having the time of our fricken lives, of course," Noah says. "Aren't we, Coley?"

I put on a smile. "You *know* it."

Eight days until Bryan flies back to the East Coast. Eight days until this weird tension disappears with him. Eight days until I can truly put that night at Whistler out of my mind.

Piper takes a step closer to Bryan. "Everything's been going good for me. It's my senior year. How are you? How's UConn?"

"Eh," Bryan says, shrugging.

"Oh, no! You don't like it? I applied there too. I mean, because my parents really wanted me to," she says quickly.

"I'm not sure it's for me," Bryan says. "When I graduated, it seemed important to get as far from here as possible. I had the right idea, I think, but the wrong place. I wish I'd taken a gap year. Or maybe two."

He wanted to get away? To me, he always made it seem like Mom and Tony didn't give him a choice. I'm not sure if he's saying this now to sound cool in front of Piper and Noah, or if it's the truth. Everything about him confuses me lately.

"I've been thinking about taking a gap year," Piper says.

Noah raises an eyebrow, which makes me think that, like me, he suspects that Piper came up with that idea exactly three seconds ago.

"That's cool." Bryan runs his hands over his hair. "Have you seen that movie *Into the Wild*? It's a true story of this dude who gave up everything, hitchhiked to Alaska, and just lived out in the wild. I'd love to do that. Unplug from the world."

"Yeah, okay," Noah says. "But what you seem to be forgetting is that that guy lived in the wild only until he *died* in it."

"Um, spoiler alert?" Piper says.

"It's not a spoiler," Noah says. "Everyone knows he died. That's why there's a movie about him."

"I'd skip the dying part," Bryan says. "I want to, like, grow a beard and just, you know, live off the land and find myself."

"That sounds so amazing," Piper says.

Noah takes my hand and pulls gently. For a moment, I resist; I know that Bryan doesn't want to be left with Piper. Then I remember that I'm not interested right now in what Bryan wants, and walk away with Noah.

As soon as we're out of earshot, Noah says, "Those two. Give me a break. They'd survive ten minutes in the wild."

My tension eases a little. "You think you'd last longer?"

"Hell, no! But do you hear me talking about wanting to kill my own food and skipping a year of showers?" He leads me into the kitchen where he grabs two coffee cups. "All right. You go in and I'll cover you."

I have no idea what he's talking about until he takes me near the champagne fountain and gives me a nudge toward it. He stands, blocking me as I hold the mugs under the cascade.

"This isn't going to fool anyone for long," I say as we slink away, each holding a full cup of champagne disguised as coffee.

"Doesn't need to." He ducks into the hallway covert-mission-ops style, and guides me upstairs into his bedroom. After closing the door behind us, he taps his mug against mine and takes a drink. "You know what would go good with this?"

I sip and shake my head.

"Some nice Cuban cigars."

"Oh, you." I give his chest a push, and reopen the door. "I think we'd better keep it like this. You know how my mom gets."

Noah plops onto his bed. "I definitely do. And now Reece knows too, right?"

I climb up beside him, careful not to flash him or catch my heels in his gray bedspread. We settle together against the pillows and face the huge, wall-mounted TV. "She hasn't let me see him since he dropped me off that day," I say. "She hasn't let me see *anyone*. I had to sneak around at the mall to get to hang out with Ming for a few minutes today."

"Harsh," Noah says.

"I know!"

"Although, with Reece," Noah says, "you should know by now that your mom is guaranteed to hate anyone she thinks wants to get into your pants. When school starts again, I think I'll tell him all about the time she found us in her closet in second grade."

I cover my face and groan. "Why do you live to embarrass me?"

"Embarrass *you*? According to your mom, I was the eight-year-old perv who wanted to show you my wang. In the dark. Because that makes sense, right?"

"You must have looked like you were up to no good," I say with a smile.

"Seriously?" Noah shakes his head. "Who automatically assumes if a kid's fly's down that it has *anything* to do with sexy times? I swear, she still looks at me funny all these years later. Reece might find it comforting that he isn't the only one. Then again, she's just getting started with him."

"Don't remind me."

Reece told me that he can handle it, that he'll try to win her over, but I don't want for him to have to. I want my mom to just be nice to him.

Noah elbows me, playfully. "You're lucky she never found out about your Latin lover."

My breath catches and I sit up straighter. "My *what*?"

"Oh, you know. Last year. You. A wedding reception. Some dude named Pedro? You'd be a lot more than grounded if your mom knew about him."

"How do *you* know about him?" I ask.

"How do you think?" Noah gulps down the rest of his cup

and reaches across me to set it on his nightstand. "I happen to
have a sister who couldn't keep a secret to save her life. And
the details of that night." He whistles. "Pretty darn graphic,
Coley, I have to say."

Humiliation floods through me.

In the shocking story that I told during Truth or Dare last
winter, supersuave nineteen-year-old "Pedro" danced with
fourteen-going-on-fifteen-year-old me during every song and
then led me back to his room where he took off my dress and
did everything to me except actual sex. The fact that Pedro is a
figment of my imagination doesn't make Noah knowing about
him any less upsetting.

"I. Cannot. Be*lieve*. Piper told you that," I say.

"You can't?" Noah asks. "If she'll spill about Felicia giving
a hand job to that bass player and Alejandra being a drama
queen about handing over her V-card, of course she's going
to tell me this, too. Why does it matter, though? She said you
told your whole fricken team."

"I had to. It was for Truth or Dare. That doesn't mean I
want everyone knowing that I'm a huge slut!"

"Calm down. You're the opposite of that, okay?" He takes
my hand. "You're a *tiny* slut."

I yank my hand away. "God, Noah."

"I'm *kidding*. Kidding, kidding, kidding!"

I take another sip from my cup, staring straight ahead at our reflections on his black TV screen. From what I can see, Noah's watching me with about 25 percent concern and 75 percent amusement. "Piper told me all of that, like, a year ago," he says. "I've never told anyone, and I never will, okay?"

"What else has she said about me?" I ask, turning toward him again.

His lips twitch. He glances at the ceiling and kind of scratches his cheek. "Um. Nothing?"

"I don't believe you."

"There might have been one thing. A little thing. Teeny." He holds his hand up with his thumb and finger about an inch apart.

"*What* did she say?"

"That you and I kissed once. Or something wacky like that?"

I chug the rest of my champagne.

"Don't worry." Noah pats my shoulder. "I didn't let on that it was news to me. It's all good."

I set my empty mug on his nightstand and sneak a glance his way. Now he's totally grinning at me.

"This isn't *funny*, Noah!"

"It kind of is."

I wonder if he'd be so amused if he were in my place, if

I were to blurt out what I've heard about him and Kimber. Something gives me the feeling that he absolutely would not.

"Look," I say. "The only reason I told them that was because I didn't want everyone to think I was a freak."

"Like the kind of freak who'd get naked with the first guy you kissed on the day of that first kiss?"

"Exactly! Anyway, it's been so long, I almost forgot that the story I told them about you didn't really happen."

"Wait. There's a story?" Noah rubs his hands together. "I want to hear it."

"No! It's embarrassing."

"Oh, come on. It was my fake first kiss too. I deserve to know how it all went down."

I let out a loud breath. "Fine. It was during freshman year when we were doing our English homework in here and eating microwave s'mores."

"I remember that."

"And you said, 'Hey, there's something on your lips.' I kept wiping my mouth and being like, 'Did I get it all?'"

"Yeah. You had chocolate and graham cracker crumbs all over. It was h-o-t-t."

"So the part that veers from real life is that you kissed me. Then you said, 'Looks like I was seeing the future.'"

Noah wrinkles his nose. "What does that mean?"

"You know, because you'd been saying 'there's something on your lips.' You were making a prediction that your lips would be on them."

"The *hell*? Why am I such a tool in your imagination?"

I can't help cracking a smile at that. "Everyone at the slumber party thought it was funny and sweet."

"You told them all that I was a really awesome kisser, right? My reputation's on the line here, you know."

"Of course I did," I lie.

"Better than Mr. Wedding Reception Underaged-Girl Seducer?"

"Definitely," I say, somehow managing to keep my smile from fading.

"What about Reece?" Noah asks. "Was I a better kisser than him?"

My face heats up. "We're always talking about Reece. I think it's time for us to talk about who *you* like."

Noah's gaze darts around the room. Outside, a firework goes off with a loud *POP!*

"Oh, boy." He gestures toward his window. "Some loser always explodes prematurely. It's close to midnight. I guess we should get out there and do that thang?"

"Smooth subject change," I say as he slides off his bed.

He pulls me to my feet. "Hey, I'm always working a few angles in Canada and the Niagara Falls area. You know how it is."

I watch him intently until he meets my gaze. "Noah, you can tell me anything. You know that, don't you?"

"All right, all right." He clears his throat. "But this has to stay between you and me, okay?"

"Of course!"

I hold my breath. I've been waiting so long for him to be honest with me.

He drops his voice to a whisper. "So the deal is, I'm starting a harem in my garage. Enjoy this time we have together because I am going to be *busy* soon."

I sigh, but I guess I can't blame him; I definitely know what it's like to not want to tell the truth.

CHAPTER 20

When Noah and I get downstairs, everyone has pretty much cleared out. Only a few stragglers are refilling drinks or grabbing their coats and wraps. We make our way through the house, out the French doors, and then stand on the porch together, looking down at the backyard. Sparkling white lights lead to the lake's edge, where everyone else is getting situated on rows of chairs to watch the upcoming fireworks show.

"So let's see. There's our moms," Noah says, pointing. "And Tony. And my dad. All parental units appear to be distracted by hosting duties, yes?"

"Yes."

"Then I'll be right back!"

He rushes inside again. I shiver at the railing and adjust my wrap as I listen to the mix of dozens of voices below and consider whether to go in and borrow a blanket.

The door opens and closes behind me, and out of the

corner of my eye, I see a glass of champagne being set on the railing. Gentle hands come to rest on my shoulders.

I don't have to look to know that it's my brother. He smells like Bryan. He feels like Bryan. I sink back for a second to steal his warmth, but then I realize what I'm doing and pull away. "Hey!" I say, turning to face him. "You startled me."

"Sorry." He takes off his jacket and places it on my shoulders. His heat and cologne are all over it and now they're all over me, too. "You look really pretty tonight, C," he says.

I pull the jacket tighter and take a few steps away from him. "Thanks."

It comes out barely louder than a whisper.

Before Bryan went away for college, I'd wanted him to stay more than I'd ever wanted anything. The little things he'd do like surprising me with Oreo milkshakes and telling me I was the coolest girl in the world would make me nearly explode with happiness. I wonder if his compliments will ever make me feel like that again.

"Have you been hanging out with Piper tonight?" I ask.

He picks up his glass, staring down toward the lawn. "Worse. Tony's been introducing me to everyone like, 'Look how great your life can be if you follow in my footsteps.' All night long, these guys have been taking turns going on and on about their awesome houses and cars and shit."

"Does that mean you weren't convinced?" I ask, wrinkling my nose.

"I'm not sure." He sighs. "I want to be, but I'm still feeling so off. I have tons of time to decide about law school, anyway. What I'm stressed about is going back to the East Coast. You know, seeing *her* again."

I nod. I hate the idea of him having to go back to where Heather is, but I also know that I need for it to happen.

The doors open behind us, and I'm relieved as Piper makes her way out, carrying a plate with little desserts on it. She doesn't have anything on over her dress to keep warm; she's definitely tougher than me.

Noah follows her with a mug in each of his hands. "Coley, here's that coffee you wanted," he says, lifting a cup in my direction.

"Yes, Noah," Piper says. "We all believe that that's coffee by the way it *isn't* steaming."

"It's cold coffee," Noah says, giving me a wink.

I hurry over and close the door behind them.

"I know you aren't big on sweets," Piper says, walking up to Bryan. "But the liquor with dark chocolate is more, like, bitter. I thought maybe you'd like one?"

"Boozed-up candy," he says. "Could be worth trying."

As Bryan takes a chocolate, Noah whispers in my ear,

"After all these years, do you think my sister has finally figured out how to seduce your brother?"

I shake my head and we step to the railing together. It's me, Noah, Piper, and Bryan, all in row. I start in on my second cup of champagne for the night.

"Are we going to be dutiful children and go down there?" Noah asks me, nodding toward the lawn while Bryan and Piper talk quietly together on the other side of him.

"Can't we just be dutiful from up here?" I ask. "I'd rather not stab my heels through your lawn."

"That's as good an excuse as any. How high are those, anyway?"

I lift one foot. "Five inches. Don't you wish I was always this tall?"

"You know you're perfect the way you are." He drapes an arm over me, rotates us toward the French doors, and smiles ahead as if we're facing an imaginary photographer. "But see how awesome we'd look in pictures together if this were your real height?"

I giggle as we turn to face the lake again. "You are *so* right."

"The Tolo dance is coming up." He nudges my arm. "No one's asked me yet."

I stare at him. He doesn't really think that *I'm* going to, does he? "I'll hope for your sake, and for the sake of your dance pictures, that you go with a tall girl this time."

"No, hey," Noah says. "You know that I'm always happy going with a certain not-tall girl."

"Umm. I kind of think that Reece might expect me to ask, you know, *him*?"

Noah's mouth falls open. "Shit! I didn't even think of that. Okay, now it's official: Your boyfriend is ruining my life."

"Oh, come on," I say, with a laugh. "You had to have known this would happen when you were giving him advice about me. Or whatever it was that you were doing."

"I *was* giving him advice. Which means he should show his gratitude by stepping aside and letting you and me continue with the streak we have going. Every dance since seventh grade. How many is that?"

I count quickly on my fingers. "Ten, I think? But no, Reece should not step aside. I mean, unless we break up. Then I'll go with you, I suppose."

Noah scoffs. "I'm your backup plan? Tell me, who was taking you to these things back when you still had that gap between your teeth? Oh, that's right. Me. And where exactly was Reece Kinsey before you got hot?"

"Alaska," I say, narrowing my eyes. "And you're being obnoxious again."

"Imagine that," Piper chimes in. "My brother. Obnoxious?"

"But she hearts me, anyway," Noah says. "Don't you, Coley?"

I put on a frown. Noah uses his hands to lift my mouth into a smile, and soon we're both giggling.

"I'd like to make a toast," Mr. Crowne says, loudly from the dock.

Everyone gets quiet and he goes into a long spiel about family, health, success, joy, and all the other sentimental stuff he likes to say at these things. Everyone applauds and drinks. Tony takes a turn and it's more of the same, followed by another round of clapping and drinking.

"Blah blah blah," Noah says as the conversations resume below us. "We should make a pact. The four of us. Right here, right now. Next year we'll do something else for New Year's."

"Like what?" Piper asks.

"Like *any*thing," Noah says. "New York. Las Vegas. Haven't you heard the superstition? Whatever you're doing on New Year's Eve sets up your whole year. I've decided that this party is the root of all my problems."

"This is only our third time coming to it," I say.

"Exactly." Noah finishes his drink and sets his mug down hard in front of him. "All of my teen years so far, ruined."

"Noah, I thought you were all about tradition," Bryan says. "Do you still kiss my sister's hand at midnight for the new year?"

"Of course," Noah says. "I didn't say I want to change that. I just think we should do it somewhere else."

Bryan says, "Yeah, but you're talking about superstition. If kissing on New Year's Eve is to make sure you have an exciting year of passion or whatever, what do you keep setting yourself up for?"

"That's a really good point," Piper says.

Noah gives me a sideways smirk and cuts his eyes toward his sister. I roll my eyes, because no, Piper couldn't be any more irritatingly obvious.

Noah and I burst out laughing again.

"Apparently, the 'cold coffee' is going straight to both of your heads," Piper says.

"Both of *my* heads?" Noah asks. "Now that you mention it—"

Piper socks his arm so hard that his eyes roll back. "Owwww," he whimpers, holding his bicep.

From the neighbors' dock, a firework goes off close over everyone below. They all duck and shriek, and suddenly I'm even gladder to be up here away from the group, even if there is only Noah and Piper separating me from the person who throws me off-balance more than anyone else ever could.

"Idiots," Bryan says.

"They do that every year," Piper says to him. "Hey, that reminds me. Do you remember that one New Year's when we babysat these two and the triplets?"

"Yeah. Nightmare," he says.

"I *know*," she says. "I always think about how freaked out we were when we set off those bottle rockets in your front yard and one of them skidded across the street and exploded in the Taylors' garage."

Bryan says, "I remember that. I also remember when you lit that lotus flower on our porch and it spun itself around, flew into the dining room, and singed our rug."

"That was Noah, not me!" Piper says.

"Listen up, everyone!" my mom calls out. "It's almost midnight. Get ready to count it down."

"Woooooooo!" Noah yells so loudly that people look up at us, laughing.

Mrs. Crowne leads the count. "Here we go. Ten! . . . Nine! . . . Eight! . . . Seven! . . ."

Noah and I scream out the numbers along with everyone else, and he grabs my hand. I set my empty cup on the railing and take hold of his other hand.

". . . Three! . . . Two! . . . One!"

I pucker up, but just as I'm about to lift his hand to my face, he pulls me forward and gives me a peck that's over and done with so quickly that I'm not entirely sure if what I thought happened really did happen.

"Was there something on my lips just now?" I ask.

"Yeah, sorry. It was the only thing I could think of to keep us from jinxing ourselves for another year."

I want to laugh because there probably would have been more passion if we'd done our usual hand-kissing thing, but instead I say, "I hope it works!"

Noah covers his hand over his mouth and makes a choking sound.

"What?" I ask.

With amusement in his eyes, he jerks his head indicating that I should look beside us.

I turn and there's Piper and Bryan: their lips connected, her arms around his neck, and his hands on her back, holding her body to his.

"Oh," I say, standing frozen, as my brain tries to work out how this completely impossible thing could possibly be . . . possible.

Noah drags me into the house and slams the door behind us in a hurry. "Jeez, Colcy! You should have seen your face."

"*My* face? What about *their* faces?"

"Pretty horrific, huh?"

Noah doubles over with laughter. I join in, and it isn't long before we're both wheezing and coughing and struggling to catch our breath. Deep down, though, I'm not sure that what I saw on the porch is all that hilarious.

• • •

After the party's over, Mom, Bryan, and I head out together—Tony's coming home on his own—and when we get to the minivan, Mom stops suddenly. "Bryan, are you okay to drive?"

"Sure," he says.

I'm not certain that I believe him. If he isn't trashed, why was he kissing and then hanging all over the girl that he's spent years insisting that he could never like in that way?

Mom pops open her bag, fishes out the keys, and hands them to Bryan. Then she looks at me. "How about if you and I walk home together?"

"Now?" I ask. "It's forty degrees and I'm wearing high heels."

"Come on." She slips her own shoes off and dangles them in front of me. "Live a little, girl."

Bryan gives me an our-mother-has-lost-it look. I could say the same for him. "Have fun with that," he says, climbing in and starting the engine up.

As I bend to unfasten my shoes, Bryan drives off.

Mom sighs. "I know you never warmed to Heather, but I sure do miss the way your brother was when she was around. I imagine it was really hard for her sometimes, though, dealing with his mood swings."

"Probably," I mutter.

I know that Mom doesn't mean any of this as an attack on me, but it almost feels like one. *Heather* made Bryan happy. For a time, she was able to change him; *she* could have saved him. Instead, she left him—broken worse than he'd been before. I can't fix Bryan, but I'm here. I don't have a choice. Still, shouldn't it count for something?

Mom and I stroll barefoot under the streetlights toward home. The sidewalk is wet and cold, but definitely not as painful as when the boys locked Reece and me out at Whistler.

"Listen, Nicole," Mom says, placing her hand on the slightly padded shoulder of Bryan's jacket as if to keep her balance. "I know you're mad at me—"

"I'm not mad."

"Yes, you are. And, just so you know, Tony thinks I overreacted too. He says I shouldn't have grounded you, that Reece was trying to do the right thing."

I don't answer. I already explained what happened with Reece and me that night—minus all the details about Bryan, obviously—but she didn't care. It's surprising to hear that Tony shares my feelings, though.

She goes on. "I know you think I'm unreasonable, but you have to remember that I wasn't much older than you when I did that exchange-student program, met Patrick, and had my entire life derailed."

I come to an abrupt stop and pull away from her. "Mom, Reece is not Patrick. Why are you punishing me just because over two decades ago, *you* chose a bad guy?"

"Don't you get it?" She throws her hands up. "I'm trying to keep my little girl safe from making my mistakes."

I soften my tone at her sad expression. "You don't need to. And the only little girl in our household these days is Emma."

"I know." She reaches over and tucks my hair behind my ear. "But you were my first, and we went through a lot together. Thankfully, you've blocked it out, but I can't forgive myself for failing you and your brother back then."

My eyes well up at the realization that she's tried so hard to protect me and has no idea that she still missed so much. I look away in a hurry, but it's too late.

"Why are you crying?" she asks.

"I'm not," I say with a sniff.

She spins me to face her. "Yes, you are. What's wrong?"

"Nothing." I choke out an embarrassed laugh. "It's just . . . you didn't fail, okay? And I love you."

"Love you, too." She wraps me in a hug, and then leans back a little to brush a tear from my bruised cheek. "Now that it's a new year, I suppose you can be ungrounded. And maybe we should have Reece over for that *Star Wars* marathon one of these weekends?"

"Before I answer, are you even going to remember that we had this talk?"

She laughs. "I had a few glasses of wine, Nicole. I might be a bit tipsy, but I'm not *drunk*."

We go back to walking and I hook my arm in hers. "Then, yes. Other than the twelve hours of *Star Wars* that I'll have to sit through, I like that plan very much."

CHAPTER 21

After I'm out of the shower two mornings later, I get a text from Reece.

> **Reece:** Is it okay if I pick you up 15 minutes early?
> Me: Yes but that means it's going to have to be a ponytail day for me.

His response comes back right away:

> **Reece:** I like your ponytails. :)

His truck pulls up in front of my house several minutes later. He's already standing on the sidewalk when I come skipping outside. I drop my bag, rush forward, and throw my arms around his waist. Almost a week has passed since we've seen each other—a strange and lonely week for me—and I don't ever want to let him go.

"I missed you," I blurt out.

He strokes my hair. "Me too. More than a thousand soft blankets. Don't ever get grounded again, okay?"

"As long as you don't ever go to Portland again."

"Deal," he says with a laugh. "And now that we've both made promises that we can't keep, ready to go?"

Reluctantly, I release him. He sets my bag under the jump seats and we climb into the truck beside each other. We've done all of this dozens of times, but now it's different in all the best ways. Now he's squeezing my hand and smiling his just-for-me smile, and I'm not wondering if or when something will happen with us; it's happening right now.

"I got you a black-and-white mocha," he says, nodding toward a Starbucks cup in the holder. "And for me, the same, but with a quadruple shot."

"Wow! Let's make sure not to mix those up."

"I'll guard mine with my life."

I can't stop looking at him while he drives. He's done something weird with his hair again and he's wearing some old-person corduroy jacket. It's all so perfect that I want to pounce on him and squish him.

We pull into the parking lot at school. He cuts the engine but leaves the radio on.

"I'm glad we left early to come to *this* place," I say, prodding his arm.

"I wanted you with me while I try to wake up before jazz band. I hardly slept last night. *Because.* I couldn't wait . . ." He sings his next words, "To see you again."

I clap my hands. "Someone's been listening to Miley Cyrus."

"Someone definitely has. And he thinks that the song 'See You Again' might be the corniest thing he's ever heard."

"What? I like it!"

"And that's what I like about you," he says. "That you can admit to that. You're fearless."

"Okay, let's talk about no fear." I tug his lapel. "What about you, going out in public in this jacket?"

"What?" he says, imitating my tone. "I like it. My grandpa gave it to me."

I rub my fingertips over the textured sleeve. "Grandpa. That is exactly the statement it makes."

"Yet you're still willing to be seen with me?" He leans in and kisses my cheek. "You really are the most courageous girl I know."

We're totally kidding around, but there's something in his eyes; he *does* think I'm brave. He's wrong, because if I were, I'd confront Bryan instead of waiting around for whatever might happen next. I can't do it, though. I can't face the awkwardness and humiliation. And the worst part is that deep down, I know that the next time Bryan tries something with me, I'll freeze up like always. I'll let him do whatever he wants. And I will *hate* myself for it. I hate myself more and more every time I don't stop him.

"You okay?" Reece touches my arm. "You look kind of bummed all of a sudden."

"I'm really tired. I was up most of the night too."

"I think we're kind of bad for each other's sleep patterns."

I rest my head on his shoulder. "I think you're right."

When I get to Gym B at the end of the day, the partition is closed, so I start my warm-up laps right away. Sometimes I have five minutes alone here in this big, echoey space, and sometimes only five seconds. Today it's something in between before two guys from the wrestling team push through the doors and head to their half of the gym. Next, Rachel S., Rachel J., and Jessica from my team come in, talking loudly. They set their things next to mine and begin their laps. Over the next several minutes, the coaches and remaining wrestlers and dancers trickle in: one by one, two by two. The louder it gets, the quicker my heart beats.

All I've been thinking about for most of the afternoon is Coach Laine and whether she'll follow through on the threats she made before vacation started. The Day of Repentance was a failure for Alejandra and me; we didn't apologize or forgive each other. In fact, I saw Alejandra in the halls a few times today, and she was always either pretending that I didn't exist or glaring at me like she wished that I didn't.

Piper drops off her stuff and runs to catch up with me. "Hi!"

Noah already warned me that Piper's been going around singing to herself like a Disney princess for the past couple of days. I brace myself for questions about Bryan. "Hi."

"I was wondering," she says, "when is your brother going back to school again?"

Without even having to pause to think about it, I say, "In five days. Saturday."

"Oh, okay."

"Why?" I ask.

"No real reason. I sent him a few texts, but I didn't hear back. He's probably busy, though. It's all right."

I clench my jaw. Piper can keep telling herself that it's

'all right' if she wants to, but that won't make it true. Bryan's known forever how she feels about him. He had to know that kissing her was going to turn into this *thing*, but he didn't let that stop him.

"Anyway," Piper says with a little shrug. "I don't suppose you've talked to Alejandra?"

I don't want to be another disappointment in her week, so I flat-out lie: "We sort of talked."

"And?"

"And . . . I don't know exactly what's going on."

I look across the gym at Alejandra, Hannah, and Liz, who are walking in together. All three of them glance up and wave. I check over my shoulder, but there's no one there.

With big smiles and swinging ponytails, they rush over to us.

"See, *that's* what Coach was hoping for," Piper says, smiling at me. "I knew you had it in you, Future Captain."

"Hi, Coley!" Alejandra says, as if the past three months never happened and she's totally happy to see me.

I'm too confused to respond.

"How was your trip?" asks Liz, jogging beside me.

"You're really going out with Reece Kinsey?" Hannah asks from Liz's other side.

"Whistler was great," I say, partially recovering. "Although we were maybe there for a little too long. And, yes, I really am with Reece."

I try to look at Alejandra for a clue about the change in her attitude, but she's on Piper's other side. The five of us continue running together in a long row.

"I'm so sorry I didn't get to meet up at Starbucks during vacation like you wanted," Alejandra says. "I was super busy. We had all this family stuff going on and it was crazy."

"Well, you *know*," Piper says. "Texting me back to tell me would have taken you about five seconds. But whatever. If things are good with you and Coley again, that's good enough for me."

A whistle blows and Coach Laine calls out, "Gather around, chickadees!"

The whole dance team heads over to stand together at the front of the bleachers where Coach is waiting. Ming waves to catch my attention and her gaze darts back and forth between Alejandra and me. I lift my shoulders, ever so slightly. Ming's mouth forms an "O" and she nods slowly, like she gets it now. Watching the realization dawning on her makes it click for me, too.

Coach says loudly, "Okay! Before we get started today, I want to check in about the Day of Repentance that we discussed a couple of weeks ago. How'd it go?" She looks around. "Anybody?"

"It went *really* well," Piper says, placing one hand on my shoulder and the other on Alejandra's as if we are her own personal accomplishments.

I'm happy to let her take the credit, but it actually belongs to Alejandra, Hannah, and Liz who put on these friendly faces specifically to fool Coach and the rest of the team.

"I think it was super helpful," Alejandra says. "It gave us a reason to talk and get everything smoothed over for a fresh start."

"We're a unified team again," Liz says. "One hundred percent."

Their smiles are huge and fake, like they're spoofing an energetic dance team, but Coach, Piper, and at least most of the rest of the team seems to be fooled by it somehow.

"Excellent," Coach says, nodding. "That was the whole point. Anyone else have anything to say?"

She looks straight at me. I have nothing whatsoever to add, so I flash a big smile too.

"All right, then." Coach claps her hands together and grins. "Let's get some stretches in and start up on your routines, girls."

• • •

It's sprinkling outside after practice. Ming and I pull our hoods onto our heads as we walk through the parking lot. Practice was intense, and with all the sleep that I've been missing lately, all I can think about is falling into bed when I get home.

Alejandra brushes past me. "You're *welcome*," she shouts over her shoulder.

In spite of the exhaustion, my pulse kicks into high gear. If she thinks I'm going to keep putting up with this, she can think again.

"You know what?" I say to Ming, straightening my shoulders. "I'll meet you at your car in a minute."

She grimaces. "Are you sure you don't need backup?"

"No, I got this." I rush after Alejandra, calling out, "Um! Excuse me. Alejandra?"

"*What?*" She turns and glares.

I put on a smile as saccharine as hers from earlier. "I think you were saying something to me?"

She crosses her arms over her chest. "What I said was, 'You're *welcome*.' Because in case you didn't know, Coach would be totally pissed at you right now if it wasn't for me."

"Oh, you're talking about that little show you put on with Hannah and Liz?" I say, gesturing toward the gym. "Don't even try to pretend like any of that was for my benefit. Coach would have been just as mad at you, and you know it."

"At least I *did* something. The most effort you could be bothered to make was having Piper harass me during my whole vacation. Nonstop calls and texts. I think I even saw her drive past my *house*—"

"I didn't ask Piper to do that stuff."

Alejandra's nostrils flare, and I realize I've said exactly the wrong thing.

There's a few seconds of silence, and then she says, "That's great, Coley. You made no effort then."

She's right. It seems that Piper's wrong about which of us would make a better captain.

"What do you want from me?" I ask. "I can't even deal with you if your whole strategy is to be fake-nice to me at practice and super-rude the rest of the time."

"I'll tell you what. Starting tomorrow, I'll aim for neutral. But *you're* going to need to come back to changing in the locker room and hanging out with the rest of us."

I look down at the cement, which is black with rain. Alejandra's and my last conversation in the locker room is what has kept me away for these past few months, and now she's talking like it's such a small thing.

"What?" Alejandra asks. "Like you can't even do that much? Come *on*."

I throw my hands up. "I'll *do* it, okay? It's a good plan."

"I'm glad you think so. Because you know that I live to come up with ways to make your perfect life even easier."

I glare at her for a long moment before walking away.

Coach Laine might be able to force us to call a truce for the team, but she can't make us be friends again.

CHAPTER 22

After my run-in with Alejandra, Ming drops me off at home where I'm greeted by the smell of something meaty and oniony cooking, even though Mom doesn't seem to be home.

I head downstairs to go to my room. *SpongeBob* is on the TV, and Bryan's on the sectional couch with his feet propped on the coffee table and his hands behind his head. I start to rush past before he can see me, but I stop short when I spot Emma lying across his lap.

I come in closer. She's asleep, wearing a red T-shirt, and is covered from waist to ankles with her My Little Pony blanket. I stare at her toes peeking out of her cast, her ponytail with most of the curls falling out of it, and then at my brother.

This bottom floor has been Bryan's and mine—our bedrooms, our bathroom, our TV room—ever since the triplets took over our old rooms upstairs when they were toddlers. Now Bryan's down here alone with our little sister.

"Where is everyone?" I ask. "What's going on?"

Without taking his eyes off the TV, Bryan says, "Tony's working late, and Mom took the boys to some karate pizza-party thing. Emma was too tired to go with them, so we're kicking back."

He's acting like there's nothing out of the ordinary here, but him spending time with any of the triplets is totally not normal. And this. Couch cuddling with Emma. This has never happened in our lives.

"If she's this tired, maybe she should be put to bed," I say, dropping my bag beside the coffee table.

"Yeah. I didn't want to wake her, though. Kid's had it rough lately."

And he started paying attention to her when exactly?

"I'll help you carry her," I say.

"Coley, she weighs, like, fifty pounds." There's an edge in his voice now. "I can handle it."

Right then, Emma sits up on the couch, stretching. The blanket slips and I breathe easier at the sight of her reindeer pajama pants. Relief at this moment is completely illogical, though, since he's had her here alone since whatever time Mom left.

Emma yawns so hugely that I can see down to where her tonsils used to be. "I'm hungry. Can we still get Jack in the Box for dinner?"

"You got it," Bryan says, smiling at her. "Ready to go?"

I say, "But isn't there food cooking upstairs?"

"So?" he asks.

"Mom left roast in the Crock-Pot," Emma says to me, scrunching up her nose. "Bryan said he'll get me something else, though. Do you want to come with us?"

I don't, but the thought of them going somewhere alone is weird on too many levels, so I agree to it.

Ten minutes later, we're in the Valley, pulling up to Jack in the Box. Emma didn't feel like changing her clothes, so she's still in pajamas and bundled up in a fleece jacket. Bryan helps her out of the backseat, and we walk with her while she slowly maneuvers on her crutches into the restaurant.

The greasy smell from the parking lot isn't as strong inside. "You get the food and I'll sit her down," I tell Bryan.

"Yes, Miss Bossy," he mutters.

At the table, I help Emma onto her chair and sit across from her. "When did Mom leave with the boys?"

"After school."

I glance over to where Bryan is standing in front of the

cash register, and then back at my sister. "So what all did you and Bryan do before I got home?"

"Watched *SpongeBob* and *Batman*."

"What else?"

"Umm." She bites her lip. "Oh, yeah. *Pokémon* one time."

"No, I meant, what else did you do besides watch TV?"

She shrugs. "Nothing."

I watch her carefully, looking for a clue about whether she's telling the truth. She doesn't seem to be acting different than usual, but that doesn't necessarily mean anything.

"Oh! I forgot to tell you," Emma says. "The doctor said that swimming might be good for me to start in a few weeks, but no karate for a long time."

"I guess that worked out," I say, trying to use a light tone.

She smiles. "Kind of."

Bryan comes to the table and sets down a tray covered with little packages of food, one coffee, and two pink milk shakes. He sits beside Emma and places one in front of her. "Strawberry, by special request," he says.

He grabs the coffee for himself, which means that the other shake is for me. I've never ordered strawberry in my life. Bryan knows better than anyone that even though the cookie pieces always clog up the straw, Oreo is my very favorite flavor.

"How's it going with the crutches?" Bryan asks, peeling off the top of a marinara packet. "Seems like you're getting steadier all the time."

Emma nods. "The problem is that people keep borrowing them. I almost peed my pants during recess because Madison wouldn't give them back."

"Next time, you have to crawl after her and take her down." Bryan grabs a mozzarella stick for himself, and then holds out the box for Emma. "For me, the only good thing about break-ing my ankle was that all these cute girls took turns carrying my books to class."

"Nobody does that for me," she says.

"Figures," Bryan says. "Fourth-grade boys are stupid."

Emma giggles and takes a bite.

I busy myself with unwrapping a burger. I don't know for sure if it's mine, but it's here and I'm here—even if my brother wants to pretend that I'm not.

I should be glad that he's being nice to Emma and not making her feel like he cares less for her because she's "just a half." Instead, I'm uneasy. He's never avoided me for days at a time. He's never deliberately tried to hurt my feelings. Watching him with Emma now—the way he's smiling at her and she's smiling back—is like seeing him with a curly haired, miniature me. The difference is that she isn't used to having his attention and I'm not used to *not* having it.

My phone chimes with a new text from Reece.

> **Reece:** *Save me! I'm stuck at dinner with my parents and this guy's asking if we had a pet polar bear in Alaska & if we could see Russia from our house.*
> **Me:** *Next he'll be asking if you lived in an igloo!*

"And there goes Coley with those texting fingers," Bryan says to Emma, rolling his eyes.

So I exist again. I tuck my phone away and go back to my burger. "Speaking of texting fingers," I say. "Are you ever going to respond to Piper?"

"You mean crazy-stalker chick? I'm thinking, *no*."

This isn't the sort of thing we would usually talk about in front of any of the triplets, but I don't care right now. "You knew that this would happen, so why did you kiss her the other night?"

"Isn't the better question, 'Why did you kiss Noah?'"

I don't know how he even could have seen that since it happened in the blink of an eye. "Technically, I *didn't*—"

"Noah!" Emma exclaims. "What about Reece?"

"It wasn't a real kiss," I tell her. "Just like the kind you'd give Mom, you know? Super fast." I look at Bryan again. "Anyway, I don't go into Noah's bathroom and put on his cologne or permanently borrow his sweatshirts like Piper used to do with you, so it's totally different."

"Wow, I never knew Piper did all that stuff," Emma says. "She's *weird*."

Bryan nods. "She definitely is."

I glare at him, and he looks away. I go back to eating without another word.

I've been in bed for two hours. I heard Bryan close his own door right after midnight, but I still can't sleep. He could get in here easily if he wanted to—there isn't a lock on my door and I'm not bold enough to prop a chair or anything under the door knob—but he hasn't tried even once since we got home from Canada.

Maybe he regrets what he did that last night at Whistler. Maybe he's scared like I am that he'll go further next time. The furthest.

Or maybe.

Maybe he isn't coming to my room because he's been going to Emma's.

I sit up.

No. He wouldn't do that. I have to believe that. He *isn't*.

What if I'm wrong, though? It started with us because of my bad dreams. Because I needed him to comfort me. Right now, Emma needs someone to take care of her. Bryan should be a safe choice because he's her big brother. But he's my big brother too, and by the time I was nine like Emma, his hands and mouth had already explored my entire body. No one would have guessed. All these years later, they still wouldn't.

I can't let it happen to her. Pushing myself out of bed, I grab my pillow, gather blankets, run upstairs, and throw myself onto one of the couches.

As I lie there and my heartbeat gradually slows, I listen to the ticking clock. There's no way Bryan will risk coming up here. Not for me. Not for Emma.

CHAPTER 23

Four days later, Tony is pouring coffee when I come up to grab breakfast at six forty-five. "Did you sleep on the couch last night?" he asks.

He already knows the answer. He caught me when I was gathering my bedding to take back downstairs this morning.

"Yeah," I say, pulling a bowl from the cupboard. "I accidentally fell asleep."

"And your pillow and sleeping bag accidentally made their way to the couch with you too?"

I don't know what to say. There is no logical reason for me to be sleeping up here. Nothing that I can tell him or anyone else, I should say. And it isn't even like this couch is super comfy or there isn't a perfectly good TV downstairs. Unless I say that Bryan and I couldn't agree on what to watch. . . .

"Don't take this the wrong way," Tony says, "but your mom

and I have noticed that you've seemed kind of run down for the last week or so."

"Thanks a lot." I force a laugh as I add water to my oatmeal packet, and put the bowl in the microwave. "I've been tired, getting back into things with school and practice and everything."

It's all true, but Reece and I have also been texting until three a.m. for the past couple of nights while I keep an eye out for Emma. Now we're both having to resort to Starbucks quadruple shots to keep from sleepwalking through school.

"You mentioned that you had a nightmare at Whistler," Tony says. "Is that still going on?"

It's nice that he cares, but I don't want to talk about this. What's going to stop him from asking me these questions? What can I say to make him put this out of his mind? Because this is over, as of this morning. It's finally Friday, and I'm staying the night at Ming's. By tomorrow night Bryan will be gone and everything can go back to normal

"I've had a few bad dreams," I tell Tony, "but it isn't a big deal."

"Maybe it is, though. Maybe it's a sign that you're stressed or, I don't know. I don't know much about psychology. But you could talk to someone. A therapist—"

"No!"

"—or your mom or Bryan?"

"The whole truth," I say, "is that I watched a scary movie at Piper's a couple of weeks ago and it's making me all weird at night." I wave my hand Jedi-mind-trick-style. "There's nothing to worry about, though. These aren't the droids you're looking for."

He smiles like I knew he would, but it fades quickly. "You've always been sensitive to horror movies and such. Maybe you should make it a policy to not watch them."

"Or maybe I should watch them *more* to desensitize myself." I pull my oatmeal out of the microwave and pour milk over it. "What time is Bryan's flight tomorrow?"

"We ended up just cancelling it. He said he brought home most of the stuff he cares about anyway, so we'll pay his roommate to ship the rest of it home."

My spoon falls from my hand and clangs on the side of my bowl. "Ship what? What are you talking about?"

"He didn't tell you his new plan? Although, I don't know if I'd call it much of a 'plan' now that I think about it. Your brother's decided he's going take classes at community college this winter and see what he feels like doing after that. Play it by ear."

"So he's staying . . . *here*?"

Tony smiles, obviously misinterpreting my screeching

voice. "See, I knew you'd be happy about it. And your mom keeps trying to tell me it might not be a bad choice, but it feels to me like he's throwing away a good thing out there at UConn."

I stare at my bowl, at the milk that splashed on the counter and my shirt, at my hands, which are now shaking. Bryan isn't leaving tomorrow. He isn't leaving at all.

"I'm surprised he didn't tell you," Tony says. "He made the final decision last night after dinner. Talk about waiting until the last minute. Well, have a good day at school."

As soon as he leaves the kitchen, I pour my breakfast into the sink and run the garbage disposal.

The boys' JV basketball game just ended, so there's thirty minutes until the start of the varsity game. Dia, Ming, Kimber, and I are by the snack stand. Tonight, the dance team is doing a rare basketball halftime performance, and we're wearing ponytails, green T-shirts, black shorts, black, green, and silver knee-high socks, and black shoes. As Ming said when we were getting ready in the locker room, we're totally *working* these outfits.

The woman hands me a coffee over the counter. I already had an energy drink half an hour ago, but it did nothing for me. Every time I close my eyes for longer than a blink, it's a struggle to open them again. If I allow myself to sit down, it's going to be all over.

Ming buys a pack of red licorice while I dump sugar and creamer into my cup. It would be better if Reece were here— I never feel this fatigued when he's with me—but he's in the gym helping Xander set up drums. They'll be playing with the pep band, so I won't get to see him until it's time to head to Vicki Lancaster's party after the game.

"Coley, you look stoned," Kimber says, closing her eyes halfway to demonstrate.

Dia laughs. "You really do."

Visine drops and concealer have been my best friends lately, but they're letting me down now, obviously.

I open my eyes as wide as possible. "Better?"

"Now you look like a speed freak," Ming says, ripping open her candy.

I sigh loudly. "It's drug-user eyes for me no matter what I do."

"We're teasing," Dia says. "Are you okay, though? You seem kind of"—she puts her hands on my shoulder blades to force my back straighter—"low on pep."

Garrison and Noah come up next to us wearing their basketball uniforms with warm-ups over their shorts.

"Unbelievable," I say, forcing a smile and some enthusiasm. "They're doubting my pep, you guys."

"And you call them 'friends'?" Noah says, with mock horror.

Garrison grins. "Don't worry, Sterling. You're a peppy chick, and we all *know* you've got stamina."

I have no idea what he means by that—and I don't think I want to know—so I say nothing.

Noah takes my coffee and brings it to his lips. "Ouch!" He hands it back in a hurry. "Where'd you get that? Out of a volcano?"

"Aren't you supposed to be in the gym?" I ask.

"Probably," Noah says. "Are you trying to get rid of me?"

"No, silly," I say, even though I kind of am; I don't like the way Kimber's looking at us.

"You shouldn't drink coffee before a game," she says to Noah. I think the tone she's going for is flirty and cute, but she sounds almost as bossy as Piper. "How about some water?" She holds her bottle out.

Noah slides his arm around me. "I'm good, actually."

"It doesn't matter what he drinks," Garrison says. "He isn't a starter or anything."

"That isn't what your mom said last night." Noah nods at Ming's bag of licorice and puts out his free hand. "Hook me up with some Red Dye Forty?"

While she's handing him a piece, I notice Garrison's gaze traveling slowly down my body. "Damn, those boots are hot," he says.

He goes on to check out Kimber, Ming, and Dia in turn, and I feel like gagging.

"Bianchi, are we going to see you and your girls at the Lancasters' tonight?" Garrison asks Dia's chest.

"Nope," Dia says.

"You might see me," Ming says sweetly. "And my girl, Coley. We'll be there with our boyfriends, of course."

Garrison looks at my face, and then at Noah's. "Of course."

The gym doors fling open and Robby from their team calls out, "Schultz! Crowne! Come on!"

"Catch you later, Sterling," says Garrison. As Noah lets me go and they saunter off together, Garrison gestures my way. "You still hittin' that?"

My back stiffens.

"Nah. Your mom keeps me too busy." Noah turns to flash a quick smile at me, but I'm too stunned to even consider returning it.

Garrison pushes him. "Shut up with that shit."

They disappear into the gym, and Dia gives a big shudder. "Bianchi feels like she needs to take a shower now."

"So does Jeong," Ming says. "What was stranger, do you think? The fact that Garrison thought our socks were boots or that he thought the so-called boots were actually hot enough to compliment?"

"And what was grosser?" Dia asks. "That he called my boobs 'my girls' or that he talked about Coley's 'stamina'? Like he would have any clue."

Ming giggles. "I think it's a toss-up."

"Garrison thinks that Noah knows about Coley's 'stamina,'" Kimber says. "It's kind of funny that Noah didn't argue."

She's acting like she's making some casual observation, but it's obvious that she's accusing me of something. "What's funny about it?" I ask. "I have a boyfriend and he isn't Noah and you *know* that, Kimber."

I sound calm—I'm sure I look calm too—but my stomach is getting tighter and tighter and tighter every second.

"Maybe you should clue Noah in to that," Kimber says. "Or do you like leading him on?"

Dia looks back and forth between us. "Meee-yow."

"Kimber, come on," Ming says.

I walk away in a hurry, and squeeze my cup so hard that the lid pops off. Hot coffee sloshes over the top, runs down my hand, and splashes onto the floor. I slam the whole thing into a trash can and keep going.

Ming catches up with me before I reach the bathroom. "Coley, Kimber's just jealous."

I turn. "And that is *her* problem, not mine."

"I know. She thinks they had a connection or something.

She's convinced herself that he'd be with her if it wasn't for you."

"It isn't true, though!"

"I know that too. So, shake it off." Smiling, Ming grabs on to my wrists and wiggles my arms around. "Kimber can suck it. Oh! Except that Noah won't let her."

She laughs at her own joke, but it's so not funny to me.

"I'm *tired* of this," I say, rubbing my temples. "I'm tired of Noah playing along with what everyone thinks they know about us. I'm tired of people having opinions at all. I'm just . . . tired."

Piper comes out of the bathroom. "Coley, is your brother here?"

"He went in the— Wait. Did you say, *my* brother?"

She nods.

"Why?" I sound almost hysterical. "Did he say that he's coming?"

"No. I just thought that he might show up."

She walks away, oblivious to the fact that her question shattered every trace of calm that I had left.

Robby makes both of his free-throw shots, putting Kenburn High solidly in the lead by fifteen points. Seconds later, the buzzer goes off and everyone on our side of the gym cheers wildly. If they can keep it up for the second half, we might win this game.

My team is already lined up at the sidelines, ready for our halftime show. Unlike our school's cheerleaders who annoy Coach Laine by standing with bad posture and talking, we keep our mouths shut and make her proud with our chins up, shoulders back, and poms in hands on our hips.

The basketball players leave the floor, and the band goes straight into "Tequila." It's been our celebration song ever since someone's parents tried to have it banned last year for being "inappropriate." We students fought to keep it and won. But tonight—even with everyone around me smiling and pumping their fists—it feels like the worst song I've ever heard.

It's taking everything I have to continue facing forward instead of turning around to see if my brother is in the stands. I let my eyes fall shut and take a deep breath. I couldn't eat at lunchtime—or all day—because no matter how hard I tried, I couldn't stop thinking and wondering and worrying about what was going to happen. I've been counting down the days, and now there's no end in sight. I have tonight at Ming's. And then what? I can't keep going like this. I can't stay on the couch forever. I can't not sleep. Everyone's noticing. Even Tony.

"Tequila" ends, and I open my eyes.

"Let's go, girls," Piper says.

We walk out together onto the shiny wood floor. The center of the basketball court is our stage. For competitions, we have tougher routines that include fewer dancers, but at the games, it's always all twenty of us together, freshmen included.

Just like the others, I get down on my knees and duck my head. Just like the others, I stand when the music comes on. Just like the others, I hop to my feet when it's my turn. We step and twirl and line up and kick, kick, kick. I'm feeling it. I'm working it.

I think I am, at least.

Turn, turn, turn. My head feels like it's spinning out of sync with my body. I miss a beat. I stumble.

Get it together, Coley.

I'm catching up. Back on track. Keep moving, keep turning. I can do this. I have to. I'm *doing* this. I can hardly breathe, but I have to keep going. We're almost done. So close.

Just like the others, I toss my poms and come to the ground in splits as the poms hit the floor beside me.

I did it. I made it. I push myself up, grab my poms, and walk slowly as everyone else jogs away. After I'm off the court and in front of the stands, dizziness overtakes me and I fall for real this time. Someone trips over me, but catches herself before she hits the floor.

Alejandra. She wasn't jogging with everyone else.

I look up, and, oh my God. I am going to die right here. Everyone is staring at me.

Without a word, Alejandra helps me up. I shuffle after her, waving at the crowd to let them know that I'm quite all right. We get to the hallway, and the rest of the team has already disappeared.

"What was *up* with you out there?" Alejandra asks, blocking the bathroom door so that I can't go in.

I look away. "Nothing."

"What do you mean 'nothing'? You kept screwing up and I had to pull you up off the gym floor!"

"Sorry for the inconvenience."

"Coley, I'm serious. Are you okay?"

Coach Laine's voice rings out from behind me. "Girls! What's going on?"

"I'm trying to get answers," Alejandra calls out. "You *had* to have seen her out there."

"Yes, I did," Coach says, stepping closer. "Coley, what happened? What's going on with you?"

I shoot Alejandra a dirty look, and then say to Coach, "I got dizzy for a second. It isn't a big deal."

"One of my dancers collapsing on the sidelines is a pretty big deal. Are you sick?" She touches my forehead. "You don't feel like you have a fever. Maybe we should have a medic check you out."

I flinch back. "No!"

"You look really pale," Alejandra says.

"I'm fine, okay? I'll be even more fine if you get out of my face."

The bathroom door squeaks open and I look over to see Kimber and Liz peeking out at us.

Alejandra purses her lips. "I'm trying to help you."

"I don't need help." I turn to leave, and Alejandra grabs my arm. "Don't *touch* me!" I yell, jerking from her grasp and pushing her hard into the wall.

"Coley!" Coach wedges herself between Alejandra and me and holds her arms up as if to ward me off. I'm practically panting for oxygen, and they're both staring at me wild eyed. This whole situation has gotten so ridiculously out of hand that I'm not even sure what's happening.

"I will not tolerate this behavior," Coach says to me through gritted teeth. "Don't bother showing up at practice tomorrow because I don't want to see you there."

"You won't," I say over my shoulder as I stomp away.

CHAPTER 24

Ming and I are beer buzzed and entertaining ourselves by singing and dancing to loud music along with a bunch of senior girls. So far, though, my first kegger isn't anywhere near as exciting as I'd expected it to be. Part of the problem, I think, is that the Lancaster house is pristine, and the carpeted areas are roped off to keep it that way. That means that lots of kids from school are hanging around, but that's about all that most of them are doing.

"They dance," Xander says, loudly, over the music to Reece. "They sing. If they can act, we'll have a couple of triple threats on our hands."

Ming laughs and takes one of the beers Xander's holding. "Sorry to disappoint you, but I'm a terrible actor."

She's right about that, although I seem to be better at it. Reece and Ming were both worried when they caught up with me after what happened with Alejandra and Coach Laine, but

I managed to make them believe that I'm totally fine. I'd probably be able to convince myself of it too, if I didn't keep catching glimpses of Alejandra and Hannah every few minutes.

"Are you ready for this?" Xander asks. "I just came up with the most awesome idea ever."

"Just like that?" Reece asks.

Xander nods. "Just like that. So I'll quit my band and you girls will become a pop duo. We'll call you . . . hmm. How about Sterling Jeong?"

"Oh, that's a good name!" Ming says.

"I know," Xander says. "You'll be known for your vocal harmonics and killer choreography, and your live show will be a huge, huge production. We're talking, like, circus-show insanity. And I'll play drums for you on your worldwide tour."

"What about me?" Reece asks.

"No offense," Xander says, "but saxophones kind of have a reputation for ruining great songs. Maybe you can learn guitar or keyboard or something?"

I step between them—in front of Reece. "As half of this duo, I want a sax player."

"You only think that's what you want," Xander says.

"No," I say. "I *know* it is."

Reece kisses the top of my head, and I sink back against him.

Xander and Ming beam at each other.

"I guess that settles it then," Ming says. "Now, will someone please tell me why this took so long?"

"What?" I ask.

She gestures at Reece's hand on my waist. "You two, with all the cuteness and public displays of affection."

"Because he had to bide his time, obviously," Xander says. "The whole school knows Coley's too cool to hook up with some geeky sax dude."

"So true," Reece says with a laugh.

I sigh. "Stop it. For real, you guys. I don't want anyone talking crap about my boyfriend." I turn and face Reece. "Including *you*, okay?"

"Okay." He takes both of my hands, steps backward until he's leaning on the wall, and wraps his arms around me. "You seem Xandered out," he says quietly.

"Kind of." I close my eyes and hold tightly to him. "Sorry."

"No, I think that happens to everyone. As long as you're not Reeced out too?"

"I'm not even a little bit Reeced out."

The music is playing as loudly as before and the room is still full of people, but everything feels so muted and far away. I could almost fall asleep right now. Literally. On my feet, sleeping. I breathe in Reece's soap-and-fabric-softener scent and focus on his heart beating beneath my cheek.

He bends and touches his forehead to mine. "You're so tired. I feel bad. I wish I'd skipped that beer so I could get you out of here."

"We can walk somewhere," I say. "Maybe to the abandoned house where we went with Xander and Ming?"

"Now you've hit delirious mode. That's a long way away, Coley."

Ming calls out from behind me, "Oh, get a room already, you two!"

"Like she's one to talk," I say.

"She actually might be onto something with that, though," Reece says. "A room sounds like it could be a quiet, comfortable, and *close* place to get you off your feet."

"Okay" I grab his hand and turn around. "Fine, Ming! We're taking your advice."

"Bow chicka bow wow," she says with a grin.

Upstairs, Reece and I step into the first open room. He flips on the light to reveal a cotton-candy pink canopy bed, and Barbies and My Little Ponies all over the place.

"Whoa. This is . . . *girly*," he says.

I nudge him in and close the door behind me. "It looks a lot like my bedroom used to. I even had the same Barbie mansion."

His lips are upturned as he glances around. "Yeah, I don't know about this. I'd feel like a really bad person, defiling an eight-year-old's bedroom."

I freeze, staring at the pink princess bed. Mine was lavender.

Reece lets out a nervous laugh. "Sorry. That was supposed to be a joke. By the look on your face, I'd say it came out all wrong."

"No. I'm fine." And I am. I flip the light off again. The room goes dark, but a glow from somewhere outside keeps it from becoming completely black. "Would this make you feel better about yourself," I ask, "if something were to, you know, *happen* in here?"

"Hello Kitty isn't staring at me, so that's a huge plus. But now I can't see my girlfriend very well."

I pull him to the bed and we sit together, with our fingers interlaced. An unexpected zing of energy shoots through me. "You don't need to see me because I am. Exactly. Right." I lean in and taste his beer and cinnamon mouth. "Here."

"Oh," he whispers. "*There* you are."

I run my fingers through his hair and he cups my face in

his hands. He brings his lips back to mine again and again. There's so much intensity in his kisses that my heart goes crazy. I want to be—*need* to be—even closer to him. I lie down and pull him onto me.

"I love the way your hair smells," he says, propping himself up on his elbows and looking into my eyes. "It's all summery like dandelions."

I wrinkle my nose. "Dandelions?"

"Or, I don't know. Daisies. Sunflowers?"

I laugh. "Those are the stinkiest flowers in the world!"

"Not to me, they aren't." He buries his face in my hair, inhales deeply, and lets out a sigh that is somehow both silly and sexy at the same time. "Have I ever told you that you're amazing," he says, "and I am so lucky?"

"I don't think I know that song."

"Not a song this time. I'm so creative that I came up with it all on my own."

I giggle as he kisses me all over my face.

Our chests rise and fall together. His mouth meets mine and my eyes fall shut and we kiss and kiss and kiss and kiss and kiss and kiss until we're both out of breath. Then we slow down and he grazes his lips against my ear, my neck, my collarbone. His hands brush across my face, run through my hair. He traces his fingers up and down my sides, slides them under my shirt. Every part of him is pressing against every part of me. My body goes limp. His hands unclasp my bra, massage my breasts. His lips press against my lips. My heart gallops. I hate that I don't hate this. His tongue probes my mouth, touches my tongue. I don't kiss him back. I don't want him to realize that I'm awake, that I have any idea what he's doing to me. . . .

"Coley?"

The voice is . . . not right.

I open my eyes and someone's face is close to mine. I slap him. "Get off! Let me go!"

Scrambling away, I fall onto the carpet and fight to catch my breath. The light flips on. I blink.

I'm on my hands and knees. Next to the canopy bed in Vicki and Brody's little sister's room.

Reece kneels on the floor beside me, his eyes open wide with shock. "Coley, what's wrong? What did I do? Tell me what I did!"

I can't believe I freaked out like that. I can't believe I hit Reece.

He blurts out, "I wasn't trying to—I promise. I mean. I thought. I thought that . . ." He tries to touch my arm, but I lean away and cover my face.

"I'm sorry," he says. "I am *so* sorry."

• • •

I've been curled up on the floor for a thousand years and Reece has been asking me the same questions and making the same apologies over and over. My panic is fading, but my embarrassment, shame, and rage are ramping up higher and higher.

This is because of Bryan. Because of how completely messed up we are. He wasn't even here and yet, he was. A normal girl would be able to make out with her boyfriend without freezing up, without losing it, without thinking about *her brother.*

Why can't I be normal?

"I didn't mean to scare you," Reece says. "I swear. I thought you were into it and—"

"I was," I interrupt. "You didn't do anything that I didn't want you to do."

He stares at me, clearly not understanding. How could he, though? How could anyone?

Reece rakes his hands over his hair and looks away. "Right at the end. I was kissing you. But it was like, you weren't there anymore."

My chest tightens. He noticed. He could feel the difference in me.

"Look." I fumble with my bra under my shirt. "I'm going outside to get some air. Clear my head."

As I stand, Reece does the same. "Can I come with you?"

"I really need to be alone right now," I say, moving for the door.

"Coley, wait."

His voice is pleading and I stop with my hand poised on the handle.

"The last thing I want is to screw things up with you," he says. "Will you just talk to me? Tell me what I can do to fix it. *Please.*"

I turn to face him. His pained expression brings tears to my eyes. "You can't fix this. It isn't even about you."

"What's it about then?"

We stand there in silence, watching each other. I can't tell him the truth. I won't. "Just forget it," I say, breaking his gaze.

"Forget *what?*"

I shake my head, pull open the door, and run for the stairs.

CHAPTER 25

When I reach the bottom of the staircase, my arm bumps Eric, who sways into Daniel, who stumbles into Kendall. She then pushes Daniel against the banister. Garrison grabs my hand, preventing me from bolting outside. "Whoa there, Sterling!" he says at the same time that Daniel says, "*Jeez*, Eckman."

Hannah, Rachel B., Felicia, and Alejandra glance up from their huddle to stare at me.

"Coley, what happened?" Alejandra asks.

I don't need to be questioned by her right now; her so-called help after halftime already caused me enough problems for one night. I yank my hand from Garrison's, fling open the front door, and escape into the cold air.

As I slam the door and step onto the stone walkway, I spot Noah leaning against one of the front pillars, talking and laughing with Brody. Noah stands up straight when he sees me and takes a few steps forward. "Hey. Um, I just got here. What's up?"

I'm nearly breathless as I say, "I need you to get me out of here."

"Why? What's going on?"

I hear the door open behind me and the roar of conversations and music from inside grow loud in an instant.

"Noah, please!"

"Okay." He nods at Brody and we run hand in hand to his car. We rush to get in and he starts the engine and pulls away from the curb. "Someone's waving like they want me to stop," he says. "I think it's Reece."

I glance over; he's right. "Just go. Keep driving."

Buckling my seat belt, I squeeze my eyes shut, but it does nothing to rid my mind of Reece's betrayed expression.

From the motion of the car, I can feel that Noah's taking the corners too quickly. "You want to tell me what's going on?" he asks after about a minute.

With my eyes still closed, I shake my head. If I talk, I'll cry. If I cry, I'll never stop. Tonight went so, so wrong and it's all my fault.

"Let's try this again," Noah says. "I'm the getaway driver, so you *have* to tell me."

I look down at my hands, folded onto my lap. The hands that ran through Reece's hair and stroked his cheek. The hands that slapped him and pushed him off me.

Noah pulls up in front of my house and parks the car. I fling my door open and jump out.

"Coley, wait!"

I run across the lawn and then stop suddenly. I can't go in there. This is the last place I want to be.

Noah catches up, puts his hands on my shoulders, and turns me around to face him. "Tell me what's wrong."

"*Every*thing's wrong! My whole life is falling apart!"

"Why? What happened?"

I shake my head again.

"Hey, it can't be as bad as you think. Whatever it is, we'll figure it out, okay?"

I'm standing on the grass in front of my house. I'm with Noah. It's dark and cold and my eyes are open. I know where I am. I know who I'm with.

I lunge forward and kiss him—really kiss him.

He doesn't kiss me back, and as he pulls away, he leaves his hands on my shoulders and steps back again to get some space between us. "Cole-*leeeeey*. What are you *doing*?"

I want the ground to open up and swallow me. I want

a hurricane to carry me away and drop me into the middle of the ocean. I want to disappear forever and ever and ever so that I never again have to see this miserable look on Noah's face.

In a quiet voice, he says, "That isn't how I feel about you. I thought you understood that."

"Of course I understand!" I shout, pushing his hands off of me. "I understand that you've spent your whole life trying to make people think you want to be with me when, really, you want someone like Brody!"

Noah's eyes widen and his mouth falls open. Without a word, he retreats to his car.

I grab at my hair and scream in frustration.

What am I doing, what am I doing, what am I doing?

I run after him. "Noah, I'm sorry!"

He keeps walking, his focus straight ahead.

"I'm okay with it," I say to his back. "I always have been. And I don't like you in that way either. I promise."

Noah turns. "Then *why* did you do that?"

"Because. I wanted to know who I was kissing for once in my life!"

"What is that supposed to *mean*?"

I look at the ground. "It means that I freaked out on Reece

tonight. He was kissing me and then I was crying. The look on his face. I can't believe it. I can't believe I did that."

"I don't get it," he says. "What are you saying? He was trying to . . . force you or something?"

"No! I got confused. Like, I didn't even know where I was. Or who I was with."

I meet Noah's gaze. He doesn't look shocked or angry anymore, just concerned.

"You have to take me back," I say. "I left my phone in Reece's truck. I have to find him and talk to him."

"No, you *have* to go to bed."

I glance toward my house, back at his car, and then at my house again. "I can't go in there. And I can't leave things like that with him."

"You're completely sloshed and you're going to make things worse. Sleep it off. Figure out what you want to say to him."

My eyes fill with tears. "I know what I want to say. That I'm sorry. And that none of it was his fault. And that I don't want to lose him. And I'm so scared that I already have."

"I'll talk to him, okay? I'll let him know that you're sorry and you'll talk to him tomorrow." He takes my arm, carefully. "Now, let's get you inside, drunk girl. You've had a crazy night."

I'm nowhere near as drunk as he seems to think I am,

but I let him lead me up the steps anyway. When we reach the front door, Noah feels around until he locates our hidden key while I stare at the tops of our shoes. "I'm sorry," I say, gesturing down to where we were standing before. "I wasn't thinking."

"I know that. But, um. Was I really that obvious about"— he drops his voice to a near-whisper—"Brody?"

"Total stab in the dark."

He lets out a loud breath. "All right. I'm going to go. I'll talk to Reece for you. Promise me you won't stay up all night watching horror movies?"

I smile weakly. "I'll try not to let you down."

CHAPTER 26

The house is quiet as I creep into Bryan's and my TV room downstairs, kick off my shoes, and turn on the television. According to the channel directory, *The Sixth Sense* is the only scary-type thing on right now. It isn't technically horror, but it will do.

I know that Noah meant the horror-movie thing as a joke. Because, obviously, I can't handle my regular life, so adding in a scary movie would push me right over the edge. But I'm determined. I am going to watch this movie.

I've caught it about twenty minutes in, so I don't entirely know what's happening. I pay close attention to the lighting, the makeup, the way the actors speak. But I find myself getting caught up in the music. My heart beats fast and I grip the blanket that's spread across my lap. I turn the volume down, down, down. Is it still scary when I can't hear anything, when I don't know what they're saying? When all I see are gray faces, hanging by ropes?

Oh, yes. Yes, it is.

"What are you doing here?"

In the fraction of a second that it takes for my brain to register that Bryan has come into the room and is speaking to me, I've already tensed up and screamed.

"Jesus!" In two strides, my brother is on the couch beside me, taking the remote, and switching off the TV. "What are you trying to do?" he asks.

I burst into tears. I wanted to teach myself to not be afraid, to not need him for anything ever again. He's here, ruining my plan, and all I feel is . . . relief.

Bryan scoots close and puts his arm around me. I let him. I don't want to, but I'm sobbing so hard now that the thing that makes the least amount of sense is somehow the only thing that makes sense. I need my big brother to make me feel better. Right now, he's the only one who can.

"You know you can't watch those movies," he says softly.

"I know," I say as my tears fall onto his arm.

"Hey, don't cry." He brushes my cheeks and then pulls me up so that I'm sitting sideways across his lap. "Don't be scared. I'm never going to let anything happen to you. You *know* that."

"I know," I say again, wrapping my arms around his neck and crying onto his shoulder.

I wish I could redo this whole day from the second I got up. I don't care what Noah says, I should talk to Reece. He deserves so much better than this. He deserves so much better than me. I need to see him.

But maybe he won't want to see me.

I cry until my head hurts, until I've used up all my energy, until I physically can't cry anymore. As my sobbing subsides, Bryan hands me tissues from the end table and then shifts us both so that we're lying across the couch on our sides, my back against his chest. I wipe my nose.

"I thought you weren't coming home tonight," he says, stroking my hair.

"I didn't mean to."

He doesn't ask me to explain. He tucks my hair behind my ear and runs his fingers up and down my arms. I close my eyes. I can't get up, wash my face, brush my teeth, walk to my room, change my clothes. I can't do anything except lie here against Bryan. Maybe if I fall asleep, he'll carry me to bed.

I imagine the voice of the instructor from my yoga video:

Let your thoughts slip away.

Breathe.

Relax.

Experience the continuous flow of breath from your center.

Close out the rest of the world.

Be at one with your inner self.

I'm breathing, relaxing. Drifting, drifting, drifting, drifting, drifting . . .

Fingers trace my ribs and startle me back to semi-consciousness. I pull my arm close against my side to try to block him from touching me there, but he slips his hand up and cups my breast in his hand.

"Don't," I say.

"Shhh," he says by my ear. "It's okay."

I awaken fully and wrench free from his arms, moving to the other side of the couch. "No, it *isn't.*"

He tries to get close to me again, but I put up both of my hands, and he stops and slumps back against the cushion. "C, what's wrong?"

"What do you think?"

I need him to tell me that I imagined the whole thing, that he wasn't feeling me up, that he's never done anything like that and never, ever, ever could. I need for him to make me believe it.

Instead, he crosses his arms over his chest and says, "I was trying to calm you down."

Oh, my God. We're really having this conversation.

I take a deep breath and let it out slowly. "Bryan, this. Us. It isn't normal. *We're* not normal. I'm your sister, not your girlfriend."

"Like I don't know that."

"Well, it seems like—I mean, the things you do sometimes. I have a boyfriend and I don't want . . . *this*."

Bryan pushes himself to stand. "Why are you turning against me all of a sudden?"

"I'm not." I get to my feet and place my hand his arm. "You know that the last thing I would ever want is to hurt you."

He shakes me off, glaring. "How would I know that? You've been a complete bitch to me lately. You wouldn't talk to me. You wouldn't even *look* at me for days."

That's the way he sees it? That this was all my doing?

"Bryan, neither would you!"

He closes his eyes for a long moment and then looks at me again. "Don't you get how much I love you? How much I need you?"

The anguish in his voice makes me feel like my chest has been kicked in, and now I'm crying again. "I love you, too. But I don't want . . . *that* with you. And I don't want to have to be scared for Emma all the time."

"Scared for Emma?"

The look on his face seems to be complete puzzlement. I hope it means that I'm being paranoid, that he has never touched her and never will. But how can I know for sure? How can I ever know anything?

He shakes his head, frowning. "Are you serious with this? I've been stuck dealing with all this school bullshit on my own, and now I try to make you feel better and you make it seem like—"

"How would *you* grabbing my boobs make me feel better? It's confusing and upsetting and—"

"And you like it. No. You *love* it." His voice cracks. "I know you do. I know how you want to be touched. I know everything that turns you on—"

"Stop," I say.

"And because of me, you know what you're into too. Like your boyfriend was going to figure it out on his own. That loser owes me a thank you."

"Shut up!" I yell.

"You like to pretend that you're so innocent, but I've been with other girls, and believe me, not one of them has ever come as fast for me as you do."

I slap his face with such force that I wonder for a moment if my shoulder's bounced out of the socket. My hand stings and throbs, but I try to hit him again. This time, Bryan catches my arm mid-swing and holds on to it. "Coley, why are you *doing* this to me?"

"Me?" I shout, pulling free. "What about you? How can you talk to me like this?"

Bryan's face is red and his eyes are wet with tears. He's looking at me like I've lost my mind right before his eyes.

"I am not the crazy one here!" I scream at the top of my lungs. "Why won't you go back to Connecticut and leave me alone?"

"What's going on?" Tony's voice thunders from behind me. My heart seizes.

I turn to look at him and I can tell by his confused expression that our voices brought him downstairs, but he didn't hear the incriminating words. He has no idea about anything, anything, anything. He never has and he never will.

"She was watching *The Sixth Sense*." Bryan wipes his eyes in two quick swipes. He sounds like he's never been so bored in his life. "I startled her and she freaked out on me."

It's amazing how easily he lies. How easily *we* lie. I glance at Tony and I can tell that he's falling for it. And why wouldn't he? Sure, it's insane that I would yell at Bryan in the middle of the night because of a movie, but the truth would be a million times harder to grasp.

I can't take this anymore. I grab my shoes and stamp my feet into them.

"We talked about this, Coley," Tony says. "You need to avoid those movies. They're not doing anything good for you."

I grab a random coat from the closet, punch my arms into it, and push past Tony.

"Where do you think you're going?" he calls after me as I run upstairs and out the front door.

CHAPTER 27

There are three routes to get to the Valley from my house: the highway, which is the quickest but also the easiest way to get caught if anyone were to come after me; the scenic way, which basically requires trudging through the forest and across the river; or the back way, which runs through a newer neighborhood of mostly condos.

I pick option three, darting behind trees and cars parked on the street the whole trek down. When I finally get to the abandoned house by Alejandra's, I feel my way up two flights of stairs. The stuff we stashed up here all those months ago to make our secret hideout more comfortable is still piled in a box in the corner.

I pull out a lantern-style flashlight and turn it on. The batteries work, so I set it on the floor to illuminate the room while I unroll two dusty sleeping bags across the plywood floor. I take a small pillow from a bag and tuck it behind my head as I crawl into one sleeping bag and layer the other on top.

The ripped plastic over one of the windows crinkles loudly as the wind whips around outside. This is the perfect setting for a horror movie, but I'm not scared of it. I'm more afraid of having to go home again to face Bryan.

Everything that he said to me was the truth. The things he's done to me over the years should have felt awful. I should have hated every single second of it. Why didn't I? How can I get turned on being touched by my brother, but be scared of my boyfriend? Why am I such a freak?

I switch off the lantern and am plunged in blackness once again. This isn't a plan. It isn't a solution. I'm hiding out in an unfinished house that has no windows, no heat, and no running water. But, for now, it will have to do; I can't keep my eyes open for another second.

Emma and I are in a dark room, and the windows are boarded up. I'm searching, searching, searching for other ways out—a ceiling vent, a hole in the floor, a hidden passage in the closet—but there's nothing.

The locks will break soon; they always break. The door will fly open.

And then what? What will happen to us?

Shoes stomp loudly. Someone's getting closer and closer. Are they coming for me? For Emma? For us both?

"Coley?"

For me.

"Coley, wake up."

My eyes flutter open and Alejandra is staring down at me. "What are you doing?" she asks.

Of all the people to startle me awake, it would just *have* to be her.

"What does it look like I'm doing?"

She takes several steps back and holds up her phone. A light flashes and there's a soft *click*.

I push myself to sit. "What the hell? Did you just take my picture?"

"Yes." Peering at the screen, she presses buttons. "And now I've sent it to your mom, Ming, Piper, and Noah."

"Why would you *do* that?" I yell.

"I'm trying to help," she says, shrugging as if it doesn't matter if everyone sees me right after I've woken up.

I want to jump up, grab her phone, and stomp on it. It's too late, though. "What do you want from me?"

"*I* don't want anything," she says, placing her phone into her coat pocket and crossing her arms over her chest. "But your mom's calling everyone. She's saying that Noah dropped you off and then you got into a fight with Bryan and ran away from home. And now you aren't answering your phone. So *she* wants you to go home. Everyone else wants to know if you're okay."

"Fine." I flop onto my stomach, wrapping my arms around the pillow. "Now they all have an ugly picture of me and can see how not okay I am, so your work here is done."

"I'm serious, Coley," she says, using a lecturing tone that makes me want to kick her. "Your mom is freaking out. She says that Tony's been driving around all night looking for you. And, apparently, Bryan has drunk himself into oblivion."

I don't want to know about this. I don't want to care. But I *do* care. "Is he all right?" I ask in a small voice.

"I'm sure he will be. It sounds like he's puke-drunk, not comatose or anything."

I squeeze my eyes shut as a mix of relief and fury floods through me. Bryan's face from last night flashes through my mind: the look of concern when he first found me watching the movie, the embarrassment and anger and anguish and confusion during our argument, the indifference when Tony came downstairs.

Remembering hurts, but it's his words that make me want to die.

You like it. No. You love it. . . .

I know how you want to be touched. . . .

I know everything that turns you on. . . .

Other girls don't come as fast for me as you do. . . .

Alejandra's phone interrupts my thoughts and then stops ringing abruptly. When she doesn't say anything, I realize that she must have silenced it instead of accepting the call. I open my eyes and study the floral-print pillowcase by my face. Daisies and sunflowers—like what Reece and I were making jokes about before I ruined everything. "What in the world is going on with you?" Alejandra asks with irritation in her voice. "You're not acting like yourself at all."

"Maybe this is my real self and no one noticed before. Why does it matter, anyway? You and I called a truce because of the team. I'm not on the team anymore, so whatever."

"Oh, come on. Coach Laine didn't kick you off. She suspended you because you were acting crazy." Alejandra waves her arms around, encompassing the room. "And look! You're *still* acting crazy. With your hair all over the place and your smeary makeup, you look like you've been on a meth binge or something."

I'd like to see her have a night like mine and wake up looking better.

"Good-bye, Alejandra." I pull the sleeping bag back over my head.

Her words come out in an angry burst. "No! I'm not going anywhere. Not until you tell me why you're so mad at me! And what happened to you to make you such a complete mess! I want answers."

I stay silent, bundled in my warm cocoon. I don't owe her anything.

Her footsteps echo, but she isn't leaving; she's coming closer. There's a loud rustle as she yanks the top sleeping bag off of me. The air shifts and then I sense that she's settling in on the floor.

"Does this have something to do with Reece Kinsey?" she asks. "Because I saw you at the party, making a big thing about going upstairs with him—"

I growl and push back the covers to glare at her. "I wasn't 'making a big thing'!"

"I saw you running away, too," she says in a rush. "You looked panicked. I couldn't help wondering if maybe it was kind of like me and Derrick? That you were totally regretting it?"

I cannot believe she wants to compare her stupid situation with mine, to make Reece out to be a bad guy like she did her boyfriend.

"Will you get off this Derrick thing?" I say. "God! I'm so sick of hearing about it."

Alejandra's back is completely straight and she folds her legs into what has to be the least relaxed version of a lotus pose I've ever seen. "It isn't like you've even been around me."

I roll my eyes. "And yet, I've still managed to hear more than enough. Even when you're not complaining, you're walking around all pathetic like, 'Poor me! I used to have a cute, awesome boyfriend, but I had no choice except to be a frigid bitch and dump him. My life is *soooooo* hard!'"

"Sometimes it *is* hard," she snaps.

"I don't feel the least bit sorry for you. So why don't you go away and be a judgmental prude somewhere else?"

Her mouth falls open. "How exactly am I being judgmental?"

"You always are! Like just now. You automatically assumed that I was alone with Reece, so I *must* have gone all the way with him. You always think the worst of me."

"I do not!" she shouts, gripping her knees.

"Yes, you do! And after you slept with Derrick, you turned it around to try to make me feel like—"

"I wasn't trying to make you feel anything. I wanted to talk to my best friend about what *I* was feeling!"

Her expression is indignant—like she's been oh, so very

wronged by me—but there is no way I'm backing down from this. "Alejandra, you specifically said, 'I can't believe you let Pedro go down on you. I can't believe you liked it.' You threw it in my face, like I'm the most disgusting person in the world."

I know how you want to be touched. . . .

You like it. No. You love *it. . . .*

"I was upset, okay?" Alejandra's eyes shine with tears. "The whole time I was with Derrick, I was waiting for him to realize he should have chosen you. I did things I wasn't ready for because I thought it was the only way he'd stay." She sniffles and tightens her mouth and cheeks as if it's taking everything within her to keep from breaking down. "I was fooling myself, though," she says. "It was never going to work."

Part of me wants to grab and shake her, but another part of me hurts for her; she threw it all away for nothing. "Derrick didn't like me," I say. "He liked *you*. Why didn't you give him a chance to prove it?"

Tears slide down her cheeks. "Because you're right about me. I am a prude. I'm a total freak and no guy should ever have to be with me. They should have someone normal. Like you."

Other girls don't come as fast for me as you do. . . .

I know everything that turns you on. . . .

"I'm not normal," I say.

She tips her face toward her lap, sobbing quietly. "More than I am."

"No!" I say, shaking my head. "I'm the freak here. Not you. I'm a screwed-up, disgusting person. I liked it when I never should have, when it was with the wrong, wrong person. And I *hate* myself for it."

Alejandra looks up, frowning. "Are you talking about Pedro? Because, okay. Maybe you shouldn't have hooked up with someone you didn't know, but that doesn't make you—"

"No. You don't understand. You don't understand at all."

She throws her hands up. "Then *make* me understand!"

"There is no Pedro!"

She stares at me. I look at the floor.

What have I done?

At least thirty seconds of silence go by, and then she sniffs. "What do you mean, 'there is no Pedro'?"

"I mean, I made him up." I meet her gaze for just long enough to see the anger in her eyes. "I lied to you. I lied to everyone."

"*Why?*" she asks.

I pick at my silver nail polish. "Because I'm a liar."

"What are you saying to me?" Her voice is rising. "You've never done anything with a guy? All of it was lies?"

"No. I've done stuff, okay? Just not with anyone named Pedro."

"Then with who?"

"It docsn't matter."

"Of course it does," she says in a shaky voice. "You must have lied for a reason. Why did you want to keep it a secret from me?"

"Because you would *hate* me if you knew. I hate myself. I hate that I'm so gross and horrible."

"Coley, who was it?"

I shake my head again. "I can't tell you."

I can't, I can't, I can't, I can't, I can't.

"Was it someone's boyfriend?" she asks.

"No," I say, even though, yes, sometimes he has been.

"Was it, like, a teacher?"

"Worse," I say.

"How much worse?"

"It's worse than anything."

She bites her lip, as if she's undecided about whether she can handle this. "Someone's *dad*?"

What I need now is for her to let this go; I've already told her far more than I ever expected to. "Forget it, okay?"

"No," she says. "I promise that I'm not going to hate you. I don't judge you all the time like you seem to think I do."

"But you will this time." My eyes fill with tears. "You won't be able to help it."

"Coley, please." She's watching me, waiting. Her lotus pose is relaxed. She's ready. She thinks she is, at least. "You can tell me anything."

Can I?

My heart pummels my chest.

I take a shaky breath and let it out slowly. I breathe again. And again. And one more time. I open my mouth. Somehow, I speak. "Alejandra, it's Bryan."

For a split second, she stares at me with what appears to be 100 percent incomprehension. Then she gasps. "You mean, your *brother* Bryan?"

"Yes," I whisper.

Her eyes are open wide. "Oh, my God!"

What have I done? What have I done? What have I done?

Clutching my stomach, I double over and lower my forehead onto the sleeping bag in front of me. Crying is literally painful right now—the muscles in my forehead, jaw, and stomach are sore from so much sobbing last night—and I'm doing it again. I'm powerless to fight it.

I shouldn't have said that to her. *Why* did I say it?

My sobs come from somewhere deep within and grow

louder and louder. My shoulders heave violently and my tears and snot pour all over while I howl.

This was a mistake. The biggest mistake of my life. I want to take it back. I *have* to take it back.

I wipe my nose on the sleeping bag and push myself to sit back up. My throat makes horrible squeaking sounds as I struggle to catch my breath. But before I can even attempt to get words out, Alejandra moves closer. She wraps her arms around me, and together, we cry.

A half an hour later, Alejandra and I are on her sleeping bag together because we've been blowing our noses on mine. I can hardly believe that she knows the secret I've been keeping for so long—the worst thing there is to know about my life—and she doesn't despise me.

I've filled her in on everything: how and when things started with Bryan, my fears about Emma, me freaking out on Reece and Noah, and the argument last night that brought me here.

"You must hate Bryan so much," she says.

I shake my head. "I don't. I love him. And I know he loves me, too. It's my fault that it turned into this big, awful thing."

"Coley, *no*. It isn't your fault."

This is the part that she doesn't want to hear, and that I

don't want to admit to. But I feel guilty, letting her blame him.

"All this time," I say, "I wanted him to stop, but I never said anything. I was scared of hurting his feelings, and I was too embarrassed to talk about it. I let it keep happening, and now he thinks that I wanted it. And I don't know. Maybe he's right."

"No! You never asked for any of that. He took advantage of you, and what he did is *abuse*."

Tears spring to my eyes, at the very idea of Bryan abusing me. "He's never hurt me. Most of the time, what he did. It felt . . . good."

"Maybe to Bryan it did."

"No," I say. "To me."

"I don't understand," she says, shaking her head. "I just watched you sobbing over this. I can tell how upset you are. There's no way you actually liked what he did."

She's both right and wrong about that.

"Remember what I told you during Truth or Dare?" I ask. "It was like that in a lot of ways. The way he touched me and everything. It turned me on. And he even made me . . . I mean, I had . . . you know?"

Her eyes open wide again. "Oh! I didn't realize that that would be possible."

I cringe. "I wish it hadn't been. But that's the thing, it did happen. And after what Bryan said last night, I'm feeling like, if I truly hadn't wanted him to do it, I wouldn't have been able to—I would have hated it more, right?"

She looks at her lap, not speaking for an agonizing moment. But then she says, "Coley, I know you said that you're tired of hearing about this, but I wonder if it's sort of like the opposite of what happened to me with Derrick. Our bodies aren't reacting the way we think they should, or the way we *wish* they would."

"Maybe?"

She takes my hand. "I think, definitely. So you shouldn't put the blame on yourself or think that you wanted it just because your body reacted to what Bryan was doing. What if it happened to Emma like that? Would you hold her responsible?"

"Of course not."

"Well, see?"

I do. I get what she's saying. I just can't make this feeling go away.

We sit in silence, our hands still clasped together. It's kind of strange because we were friends for so long, but we never felt the need to do this before. It's nice, though, having her to hold on to.

"I'm really sorry," I say. "I wish I had been there for you

after what happened with you and Derrick. I wish that instead of avoiding you, I'd done something to make things right."

"Me too. But I understand now why you reacted the way you did." She takes a clean corner of the snotty sleeping bag and wipes my cheeks again. "What are you going to do now? You're not safe at home."

"I'll be fine. I'm pretty sure that after last night, Bryan won't ever come near me again."

"But what if he does? You shouldn't have to worry all the time. You shouldn't have to keep this secret. And what about Emma?"

I shake my head. "He was shocked when I mentioned her. I don't think he'll do anything."

"You don't know that, though," she says. "You have to tell your parents what's been going on."

"I can't."

She squeezes my hand. "Coley, you need help. And Bryan needs help."

"It'll ruin everything, though. Can you imagine what this will do to my mom after what she's been through? It'll destroy her."

"She needs to know. It's destroying you—"

"Coley?" A familiar voice shouts from downstairs. "It's Reece! Are you here?"

"I can tell him you aren't ready to talk," Alejandra says in a whisper. "Unless you think you are?"

"I think I need to," I say.

"Okay." She runs her fingers through the front of my hair, tucks it behind my ears, and then gets up off the floor. I listen to Reece's shoes making their way up the lower staircase.

"Coley?" he calls out again.

Alejandra heads down, out of my view. "She's up here!"

A few seconds later, Reece comes to the top of the stairs, and we stare at each other from across the room. His stance is guarded, and so is his expression. I don't know how to fix this, or if it can be fixed. There's too much to say. Too much that I don't know how to say.

For over half of my life, I've been pretending that my brother doesn't really do the things he does to me. Reece keeps trying to put the pieces back together without having any idea what's causing me to break.

I push myself to stand. He meets me in the middle of the room, folds me into a quick hug, and then takes a couple of steps back. I want to cling to him, but I know that it wouldn't be fair after everything that's happened.

"How'd you know where to find me?" I ask.

"Ming forwarded me a picture. It looked like it could have

been taken here." He hands over my bag. "After you left, I tried calling you a few times. Later I realized that your phone was buzzing right behind my seat. You should probably check it. It's been going off all night."

"Thank you," I say softly.

He nods.

I dig the phone out and scan my notifications: seven new texts from Ming, three from Reece, two from Noah, one each from Tony and Piper, as well as several missed calls from Reece and my mom. Nothing from my brother.

I tuck my phone back inside and let my bag drop onto the floor.

"Are you okay?" Reece asks, taking a step closer.

I look up at him. "No. And I'm sorry for that because you don't deserve this craziness."

"Noah talked to me after you'd gone home. He kept saying you were drunk. But that wasn't really it, was it?"

I shake my head and my eyes get watery again. "I have some things to figure out. I never should have dragged you into my screwed-up life. I'm so sorry. For everything."

"Coley, you didn't drag me anywhere." He brushes a tear from my cheek. "I'm here because I want to be."

Last night I pushed Bryan and slapped his face. I told

him to leave me alone. I ran away and didn't come back. But before any of that happened, I did all of those same things to Reece. Unlike Bryan, Reece sent texts and tried to call. Unlike Bryan, Reece came looking for me. Unlike Bryan, Reece didn't deserve any of it.

I throw myself at him and put my face against his chest. He holds me close. Maybe someday I'll be able to explain this to him. Part of it? All of it? I don't know. I don't know anything except that I'm so glad he's here.

CHAPTER 28

After I've had Reece go home for some much-needed sleep, sent a couple of quick apology texts to my friends, and washed my face at Alejandra's, she drives me home. She already called my mom for me, to let her know we're on our way.

As we pull into the driveway beside Bryan's car, my whole body tenses. He's inside the house now, and soon I will be too. And then what will happen? It isn't like we can "go back to normal." That's something we've never been.

"I'll come in with you, if you want," Alejandra says, putting her car in park.

I know she thinks that me telling the truth is the only thing that will truly end this, but I'm not sure I have the strength.

"It's Saturday," I say. "You have to get to practice."

"I'm not worried about that right now. If you need me, I'll stay."

I shake my head. "I'll be all right."

"If you're sure. I told your mom that she should let you talk first instead of yelling. Who knows, maybe she'll listen?" Alejandra reaches across the seat and we hug. Yesterday, at this time, neither of us could have guessed that this would be happening. But here we are.

"Thanks for finding me," I say, opening my door.

She gives me a little smile. "It wasn't hard. That's where I would have gone. Call me later?"

"I will," I say.

"Promise?"

"Promise."

I wave as she drives away, and stand on the sidewalk staring first at Bryan's car, and then at the house.

When I get inside, Mom and Tony are going to have questions for me: *Where have you been? Why did you run off like that? What is going on with you?*

I have lots of answers prepared in my head; I just don't know which ones I want to say to them.

The front door opens and Jacob yells over his shoulder, "Coley's home!"

Not much time to decide now.

Within seconds, Mom comes rushing down the steps in her bathrobe and slippers. I can barely feel my legs, but I think they're taking me toward her.

We move closer and closer to each other, and my heart beats faster and faster.

I have options here. I can lie about why I left last night. I can keep pretending that nothing's happening. I can turn and run away forever.

But for the first time in my life, none of these choices feel like the right one.

I'm ready to let her know the truth.

Finally ready.

I look into her worried eyes, take a deep breath, and let it out slowly. "Mom," I say. "There's something I have to tell you."

RESOURCES FOR HELP

RAINN

(Rape, Abuse & Incest National Network)

www.rainn.com

Pandora's Project

Support and resources for survivors of rape and sexual abuse

www.pandys.org

MINDI SCOTT is the author of *Live Through This* and *Freefall*. She lives near Seattle, Washington, with her drummer husband. Please visit her online at mindiscott.com.

DATE DUE

0